The Dogs that Follow their Detective Dreams # 2: The Mystery of the Stolen Gemstones

By

I0543698

Sarah Cantu

Second Edition, 2007

The first edition was written from July to
November 23 of 2006. Story typed and edited
from November 24 to December 27 of the same
year. The second edition was produced during
June and July of 2007.

Dedication

This story is dedicated to all my friends and companions at Kingsway Christian School and to people who have read my books! Everyday affects and adds ideas to my inspiration to come up with these wonderful canine tales of mystery, humor, fun, and teamwork!

Special thanks to my publisher, editor and Dad, Ricardo Cantu, my encouraging mom, Veronica Cantu who enjoys all my stories and the music I compose! I hope to keep on writing, keep on composing, keep on singing, keep on playing music, and keep on doing everything that helps to improve my talents!

Special thanks to Syloria my poodle! Even though I no longer own you, you sure did make a difference and inspired me to create the main character of the Dream Detectives Dog Club, Syleria Susae along with helpful pointers on creating the other seven dogs with all their little personalities!

Contents

Prologue:

Part I: Mario Marco

"You owe me $500!" screamed Allie Angie with delight as Gabriel Gordon handed her some yellow colored bills. You could see that he was not happy. "It's my turn now!" exclaimed Syleria Susae. She rolled the two square shaped dice and moved her token to Chance. She picked up an orange card, "Oh no, I have to pay each player $50!" She handed each player a blue bill. I know, you are probably wondering what is going on. I'm Mario Marco, a 3 month old brown standard poodle. My friends and I were playing monopoly in our apartment. Our neighbors had to work, so they let our friends come over for the day. Our apartment is located in San Francisco, California.

Today was July 28th, Tuesday at 3:35 in the afternoon. It was cloudy outside and the sun was definitely not shining. Obviously, you are most likely wondering who

we all are. Well, I'll explain
that when you flip this page and
move on to the first chapter!

Chapter 1: The Dream Detective Dogs Club

I already introduced myself as Mario Marco, so I will tell you a little about my friends. My ultimate buddy and companion is Syleria Susae. She is a Dalmatian who has not developed her spots and has the same age as me: three months! We were adopted by two nice people, Mr. Maxwell Louis and Mrs. Lydia Louis. Our neighbors are Daniel and Kimberly McMartin.

My other pet friends are Royal Romeo, Pierre, Allie Angie, Gabriel Gordon, Delilah Mara, and Vanessa Pana. Royal Romeo is a Dalmatian who used to be a working dog at a hotel. He is 2 months old. Pierre is a 4 month old Dalmatian whose owner died less than a month ago. Pierre at that point, lived in an old garbage dump.

Allie Angie is a 5 month old Dalmatian and Gabriel Gordon is a 4 month old black toy poodle. Both of them were rescued from an Animal Control Center.

Delilah Mara is a 3 month old silver minature poodle and Vanessa Pana is a 6 month old pink standard poodle. (Her fur color is really white, but her previous owner dyed it pink!). They both were rescued from a Humane Society when they were about to get euthenized and sent to their painful death.

Mr. and Mrs. Louis did not adopt Gabriel Gordon, Allie Angie, Royal Romeo, and Delilah Mara, but gave them to our neighbors who live next door to our apartment. We pets see each other at least two or three times every week. Syleria Susae is the president of our club, The Dream Detective Dogs Club. I am the vice president. Our secretary is Delilah Mara and our special extra clue explorer is Pierre. The rest of us dogs are officers. Delilah Mara keeps track of our mysteries in a special club notebook. Pierre brings, shows, or records clues. The officers help too sometimes. But that is not the end of it. Syleria Susae has an aunt named Sheryl Star. Delilah Mara has a cousin named Jackson. Sheryl Star and Jackson have friends and a club of their own called of their own: The Feline & K9 Companions.

Mr. and Mrs. Louis are actually aunt and uncle of a girl named Sadie Dawes. She has two dogs, Sheryl Star and Jackson, and three cats, Panda Perry, Rosie, and Halloween. (Read the Feline & K9 Companions series.) I would tell you everything about them, but my main focus for this tale is a mystery solved by us: The Dream Detective Dogs Club!

Chapter 2: A Festival!

Before I introduce you to our mystery, I'll mention some of our previous sleuthing experiences. They won't seem much like mysteries to you though. It all started when we heard about the Feline & K9 Companions. Because they were famous in the State of California and Western part of the U.S, that amazed us. Our club was started because each one of us, including me, was influenced by those modern sleuths. We thought that could help us become famous too and maybe mystery solving could become a new hobby!

But lately we hadn't turned up with anything unusual. Our first few mini mysteries we started off with were random and as I said, weren't much of mysteries:

1. *Finding Syleria Susae's Missing Bone*

2. *The Mysterious Finding of the White Glob Monster*

3. *Old Spider Webs in the Bathroom*

These mini mysteries were recorded in Delilah Mara's special composition notebook. Ok, our first mystery: Finding Syleria Susae's bone. In the end we had figured that that wasn't much of a problem. The truth was the bone was misplaced in Mr. Louis's underwear drawer instead of Mrs. Louis's sock drawer.

Our second sleuthing mystery was like the one I mentioned above. There was really no glob monster since that's what we thought in the first place. Our glob monster was actually gravy that had been overheated in the kitchen microwave. Mrs. Louis had put in a pot of gravy in the microwave and had gone to take a quick shower while the gravy got warm for her stew which she had planned to make for our dinner later on. But during her process of setting the timer for the gravy, she put it for 30 minutes instead of 3 minutes. I know that sounds like a lot to heat up gravy, but it was frozen and Mrs. Louis couldn't add frozen gravy to her recipe on her stew.

While Mrs. Louis went off to tend to her shower, Allie Angie had been in the kitchen washing dishes when she started hearing sudden movements in the microwave. When she turned around, she saw whitish acid slithering and banging against the microwave door. The sight was horrifying to her I guess because she called us all over to the kitchen.

The whole club rushed in the kitchen to investigate the strange moving creature in the microwave. When Syleria Susae took a look at that gravy, her face turned green and she looked like she was about to throw up. Delilah Mara couldn't stand the smell of it for she backed away and refused to come to the microwave until we turned it off. But we were all too excited and curious about the moving gravy that we sort of ignored her offer. I had taken a magnifying glass and taken a good look at the gravy. It looked like lava and bubbles.

Chapter 2: A Festival!

"Cool!" I exclaimed. "Ew! Gross!" screeched Vanessa Pana who had taken her first look.

The gravy had been boiling excessively in the microwave for about 20 minutes when we heard Mrs. Louis came rushing out of the shower with a heap of towels. "Oh my goodness! The gravy's exploding!" she cried. Right away she turned off the microwave and with oven mitts, carried the bubbling bowl of white stuff. When she opened the microwave door, a horrible nasty smell came pouring out along with clouds of smoke and whitish fog. For once in my life, I saw evaporation! People have told me that water can evaporate with the sun's warmth. But it never occurred to me that the same could go for gravy. The awful part about this incident was that it brought a negative outcome. From that point Allie Angie refused to warm up her beef loaf in the microwave until we had proof that the food was not a living thing.

Finally, our last mini mystery was the old musty webs in the bathroom. The situation was we never knew that webs came from spiders. Every time we would go in the bathroom to brush our fangs and teeth twice a day, we would find a crowd of scurrying spiders rushing out of the bathroom. Behind the toilet, on the shower curtain, on the sink, and near our toothbrushes were webs!

One day Pierre and Royal Romeo decided to investigate where these webs were coming from. One evening before dinner we stayed in the restroom and hid behind a couple of wastebaskets near the sink. After we went into hiding, we noticed a small group of spiders coming from all directions toward the bathtub and the toilet. Second by second, their spinnerets let out sticky string like threads. The spiders worked for almost an hour on their masterpieces. When they were finished, there before us were webs! The same type just like we saw before! Our mystery was solved! All we needed to do was add bug spray to Mrs. Louis's shopping list the next time she went to shop at the store! Even

Mrs. Louis seemed to have gotten annoyed with those creepy crawly creatures.

One day while Mrs. Louis went to the groceries store, we called the whole club together and waited for the arrival of the spiders. When we saw the first few web makers appearing at the entrance of the bathroom, Syleria Susae, the president of our club made a peace treaty with the spiders. Syleria Susae would promise they could make webs in the attic if they would stop their web making process in the bathroom. Those little bugs nodded their tiny heads in agreement. I went upstairs to open the attic door a crack so the spiders could go through. Two weeks later, I went up in the attic to see how the spiders were doing in their new home. The whole attic appeared to be full of webs. But in these webs were web made words from the spiders. One web had huge stick like letters that read: Thank You!

I'll tell you a few last things about me and my friends. Vanessa

Pana is the oldest of our group. She is a talented artist. Her personality is considered to be sweet, gentle, and kind. I think she's the type who loves to take life easily. Allie Angie is our next dog whose age is 1 month behind Vanessa Pana's. Some of her hobbies include racing, writing stories, and playing sports! Gabriel Gordon is one of my best pals. It's unusual, but his passion is learning and filling his mind with education from a human's point of view. Since he's gotten into science and chemistry lately, his future plan is to be a pharmacist who will construct the first pharmacy for canines. Pierre is a buddy of Royal Romeo. They like working together on lots of things. Pierre's personality is described as energetic, bold, and brave. One puppy game he enjoys for passing the time is "pirates!" I think the most organized dog in our club is Delilah Mara. But in some ways she gets us annoyed with her attitude because she seems to be curious about EVERYTHING! To keep track of her comments, she owns a secret notebook (not our club notebook) where she writes all sorts of stuff. On some nights when she's asleep, I quietly read what is written in her notebook. You would be surprised at how much she can write. It's one word per three seconds to be exact; practically a new world writing record! I bet even Ann M. Martin can't write that fast even though she publishes about a book every year. Delilah Mara reminds me of the fiction character, Harriet the Spy. Finally, Royal Romeo, Pierre's friend is hilariously funny! He just loves reading joke books. Especially Garfield and Calvin and Hobbes!

Tomorrow is going to be July 19th, Wednesday! Royal Romeo and I are writing in a notebook (the club notebook). But here's what is happening: I'm a horrible speller. If I ever compete in a spelling bee, I would be disqualified at the first word or maybe the first letter! I'm so glad that dogs don't go to school or else I would probably fail all my spelling tests and always get pulled back to first grade. This is what we wrote:

July 19th, Wednesday – 8 p.m.

Mario Marco – I think the musium's speshul event mite bee sumthing we coud look forword to. Don't u think Royal Romeo?

Royal Romeo – What's awesome about it is that they're celebrating the rescue of the stolen gemstones which were found.

Mario Marco – We will probubly be iggscited about this!

Today is July 19th as you can see. In our county we have a local building called the San Francisco Prehistoric Museum. It recently opened up a new exhibit called the Valuable Rocks Exhibit. It contains gemstones and meteorites. They were stolen last month but later found by the Feline & K9 Companions. (To know more, read the Feline & K9 Companions # 1: The Mystery of the Stolen Valuables). Now the museum was having a festival for the bravery of the famous detective team. But some of the members were away on a biking trip in Texas, so the festival would be held at the end of the month.

To tell you something, the Dream Detective Dogs are able to talk to their owners, but not to anyone else. Well, maybe the neighbors and the Feline & K9 Companions, but that is if we ever meet them someday. Nobody other than these people should know that we can talk. This is what happened when our owners mentioned the festival.

"I know, let's go to the festival!" yipped Pierre. "But we would have to ask our owners first," reminded Syleria Susae. That was exactly what we would do. In the end our owners finally agreed to the idea! The festival would be held at the end of the month on the last day of July! That night, when everyone was asleep, I peeked into Delilah Mara's secret notebook to see what she had written for today. What I read were some of the weirdest comments I had ever seen in

letters (Well, duh. Her comments
are always weird):

ROYAL ROMEO HAS BEEN HIGHLY TOO
ENERGETIC! IT IS EITHER THE JOKE
BOOKS HE'S BEEN READING, OR IT IS
THE CAUSE OF PUTTING TOO MUCH
SUGAR IN HIS CEREAL.

That was normal. Delilah Mara
always wonders about Royal Romeo's
funny humor.

PIERRE LOOKS SORT OF SMALL FOR A
DALMATIAN. IF I WAS THE FOUNDER OF
THE DALMATIAN BREED, I WOULD
CATEGORIZE SMALL DALMATIANS AS
LITTLE TEENY TINY SPOTTED
CHIHUAHUAS.

Well, that was a new one. Delilah
Mara has never mentioned anything
about Pierre before.

IS SYLERIA SUSAE REALLY GOING TO
GROW SPOTS LIKE HER AUNT AND MOST
DALMATIANS? IF I WAS THE PRESIDENT
OF THIS CLUB, I WOULD PUT HER AS A
JUNIOR OFFICER.

That one sounded mean. But who
cares? If Delilah Mara is going to
be that way, she can.

Chapter 2: A Festival!

I WONDER IF MARIO MARCO HAS BEEN
EATING TOO MUCH. HE PROBABLY HAS
PUT ON SOME X-TRA WEIGHT.

Sheesh, Delilah! Sometimes I wish
you could keep your comments to
yourself, in your HEAD!

DO DOGS GET PIMPLES? IF SO, ALLIE
ANGIE HAS ONE ON HER EAR. I HOPE I
DIDN'T MISTAKE THAT FOR A WART. DO
WARTS COME FROM FROGS, OR TOADS?

That was enough looking
through Delilah's notebook. I
turned out my nightlight and went
to bed. There was frightening news
the next few days, but who knows?
Maybe our club can solve a crime
like Syleria Susae's aunt who is a
member of the Feline & K9
Companions! Delilah thinks that is
impossible, but she is sort of
stuck up at times. For now, I
wished that she would keep her
thoughts in her brain instead of
writing them on sheets of paper.

Chapter 3: Saturday Beginnings

July 23rd, Saturday: 9:00 a.m.

<u>Allie Angie</u> – This is horrible! The gemstones were stolen again!

<u>Mario Marco</u> – U don't think it coud bee Vanesa McAttee, doo u?

<u>Allie Angie</u> – She did steal them the last time, but she's in jail now ever since last month.

<u>Mario Marco</u> – U maye nevver be shure, Ally Angy.

<u>Allie Angie</u> – You spelled my name wrong.

<u>Mario Marco</u> – Whoops, sorry about that, Allie Angie.

<u>Allie Angie</u> – It's okay. But if it is Vanessa McAtee, we'll catch her this time, even if nobody thinks we can.

<u>Mario Marco</u> – R U up to sumthin?

<u>Allie Angie</u> – Yeah! This could be our first official mystery that could help us prove that we can be as good as the Feline & K9 Companions.

Chapter 3: Saturday Beginnings

<u>Mario Marco</u> - Cum on, Allie Angie! Wee hav a mistery to solv.

I think I would say that today was horrible at first. It became that way when we realized that the Prehistoric Museum's gem stones were stolen! At least the museum's four meteorites were safe! This was not the first time they had been stolen though. The last time they disappeared, they had been taken by Vanessa McAtee, a neighbor of one of the Feline & K9 Companion members, Christina Norman. Vanessa McAtee became a suspect when she showed curiosity about the gemstones and was more than eager to find out about the meteorites.

This morning, I was watching the news. My owners were working at their jobs, so I never told them until later. It all started when a news reporter I heard on TV reported: "Attention to all California citizens! We have recently received a report from the Prehistoric Museum! Our gemstones were stolen again! Fortunately our meteorites were

still secure in the exhibit. We
need detectives who will help us
once more on this case. It worked
the last time, so it should work
this time. If you have any
information on these stolen items
or want to help volunteer for our
detective sign up, call this
number:

1 - 888 - PREHISTORIC - 123

Or go to the San Francisco
Prehistoric Museum!"

Pierre was also watching the news
with me and he ran toward me and
yelped, "Mario, We have to do
something! We can't let the museum
down!" I looked at Pierre for a
long time with a surprised look,
"If it's for a museum that needs
our help, we might as well." I
called over Syleria Susae and
Vanessa Pana. I told them right
away what happened. When we were
all settled around the dining room
table I asked, "Syleria Susae, do
you think your aunt, Sheryl Star,
could help us solve this mystery?
She's an experienced, professional
detective!" Syleria Susae's happy

expression disappeared and she said quietly, "I wish she could, but her Feline and K9 Companions Club is on vacation and is taking a break from solving mysteries. I don't want to spoil any of their schedules."

Because everyone seemed so sad at that point, Pierre tried to make things more positive by suggesting, "Maybe WE could solve the case!" At that point, Allie Angie, Gabriel Gordon, Delilah Mara, and Royal Romeo came over just then and we told them about the bad news. Right away, gloomy expressions formed over their faces. Pierre said, "I didn't mean for everybody to get so sad in a couple of seconds. I have an idea! Let's take a vote. Who does NOT want to be super sleuths for this mystery?" Vanessa Pana, Delilah Mara, and Gabriel Gordon raised their paws. "Who thinks my idea will work?" Pierre continued after the first few votes? Everyone else's paws went up in the air.

After the votes were counted, Pierre announced, "The vote beats five to three! We start now and solve the crime!" Everyone started to cheer, "Yea!" Because the museum wasn't too far away, Allie Angie, Delilah Mara, Gabriel Gordon, and I went to the museum! The others stayed home just in case our owners would arrive home early. Even though they usually don't, you may never know.

As we walked several blocks to the museum, I noticed a couple of things: First, Delilah Mara and Gabriel Gordon were both carrying notebooks! (Delilah Mara hardly ever takes her secret notebook out in public.) Secondly, other people seemed to be heading to the museum too! When we arrived, there were large crowds of people. "Why do you both have notebooks?" Allie Angie had finally asked Gabriel Gordon and Delilah Mara. I could see that she couldn't take it any longer. "For taking notes," said Gabriel Gordon. "And comments," continued Delilah Mara shortly. "Wow, another episode of Delilah Mara's unusual comments," I thought to myself.

The Prehistoric Museum has five floors. The truth is, the museum was constructed to look similar to the Children's Museum in Indianapolis, Indiana. If you compared the two museums, they have similar floor plans. Their new exhibit is obviously on the top floor. When we entered the museum lobby, there were lots of news reporters and camera people. I looked through the crowd and on a wall near a bulletin board was a huge sheet of paper. Some people were signing their names on it. "This must be the detective signing sheet," I said to myself. Quickly I called my friends over, "Allie Angie, Gabriel Gordon, Delilah Mara, over here!" My friends jumped right over to me and read through the list of people that had recently signed up. We saw more space near the bottom of the sheet which was blank. I took a blue pen and wrote: Mr. and Mrs. Louis's Dream Detective Dogs Club.

After that, we took the elevator to the top floor and explored the exhibit which was half vacant. As we walked around and studied the empty exhibit structures, I saw Delilah Mara doodling notes in her secret notebook. Oh, Delilah! It seems like you want to write more than solve. But as it usually is, she adds more unusual notes to her notebook:

I THINK THIS MUSEUM NEEDS A BETTER SECURITY SYSTEM. DON'T YOU THINK?

I DOUBT OUR CLUB WILL SOLVE AN OFFICIAL MYSTERY. JOBS LIKE THIS ARE 4 BIG PEOPLE (& ANIMALS) ONLY! BY THE WAY, I'M NOT INTERESTED IN BEING A NANCY DREW II. DOES ANYONE IN THIS TOWN AGREE WITH THAT?

I looked over at a couple of the gemstone display stands. They were definitely empty! At that point, I heard a voice behind me and turned around, surprised to hear a girl say to an employee, "Too bad the gemstones were stolen. I wanted to actually study them for my book report." The girl looked like a young teenager, 15 years old. Her hair was curly and short (probably up to her chin).

"Don't worry Marie, we'll try to get those treasures back!" replied the voice of another girl who was about 13 years old and had long blond hair that went past her shoulders and down her back. "How can you tell, Suzanne? We'll never be rich detectives like the Feline & K9 Companions!" cried the first girl. My attention was drawn away from those girls to an employee at the entrance of the exhibit who announced, "We're drawing names for three detective groups tomorrow at 4:55 p.m.! Come and see if you have won at the announced time!"

Chapter 4: The Three Chosen Groups and a Lost Bracelet

That night, we told our owners about Pierre's idea of solving the mystery and how we entered our group in the museum detective sign up entry. "That sounds very exciting!" exclaimed Mrs. Louis. "Maybe I can take a day off from my job and help you young detectives!" he suggested. The next day we went to the museum to find out who would be the three ultimate detective groups.

July 24th, Sunday - 5:37 p.m.

<u>Mario Marco</u> - I'm suspishus ubowt that teenage gurl, Marie. I wunder how her bracelet wuz left in the rooby displaye stand.

<u>Royal Romeo</u> - Who knows? But I wonder if Vanessa McAtee is at it again.

<u>Mario Marco</u> - It could be one of those too people. It's weerd, but I wunder if Vunessa MicAttee could ever get out uv jale.

<u>Royal Romeo</u> – I doubt that, Mario Marco. She'll be in jail for quite some time.

Allie Angie, Royal Romeo, Syleria Susae, and I, (along with Mr. Louis) went to the museum to hear the upcoming announcement. I was sitting on a small checkered colored bench watching some more people sign up for the detective entry, when I heard familiar talking. When I turned toward another direction to the ticket booths, there was Marie, the suspicious girl who I had seen yesterday. "What was she doing here?" I thought. It took only a couple of minutes to notice and recognize some of her outer features. For one, she seems to be a very social person (probably a popular girl). Marie was chatting with three other teenager boys about her age. Yep, she's 100% popular or else those guys wouldn't be looming over her a lot. Her hair had tight curls at the end like a sheep. I wonder what salon she goes to. Maybe Pink's Petit Makeover. It was only four blocks away and they have some of the trendiest and weirdest hair cuts, perms, highlights, and styles you have ever seen!

Her ears had gold colored hoop shaped earrings and one pink bracelet with extremely red jewels. They gleamed and shone so much that I started to wonder if they were even real. I saw other teenagers crowd around Marie and admire her beautiful bracelet. But Marie would not let them touch her bracelet. That was awkward though. If I were her, I would let people take a closer look at my own jewelry. Even though I'm not interested in jewels and girly stuff, that would be a more polite way to act around peers. I took a few steps toward Marie until I was barely three feet away from her. I took in a breath and sniffed. A cloud of dust surrounded me and I sneezed. "Whoa, this person put on too much perfume," I thought as I coughed over and over again. I tried getting away from the perfume smell, when a voice over a microphone caught my ears, "Go to the main lobby within 10 minutes to see if you have won the prize

to our detective sign up entry!"
I heard another familiar voice
within the crowds of people. It
was Mr. Louis!

"Come on, Mario Marco! We
don't have much time left and we
need to be on our way to the
lobby," he said. He gathered us
all around and led us to our
destination. In the lobby was a
table with a bucket and many
people! Inside the bucket were
pieces of folded paper. I guess
those had the names of the people
who signed up. In a moment, the
museum manager stepped forward and
behind the table. He announced,
"Attention everyone, I am glad you
have all come at this appointed
time to see who is lucky for our
grand prize: Three groups of
people or animals that will aid us
on our find of the stolen
gemstones. I am sorry if you are
not picked, but the museum only
needs three detective teams. Those
teams whose name is called out
will come to the exhibit and
examine the place for any found
clues. So let's start by reading
off these names!" A roar of cheers

came from the crowd of arriving people. The manager stuffed his hand in the bucket. "I hope we win!" exclaimed Allie Angie excitedly. "I am pretty sure we will!" replied Royal Romeo. The manager's hand held a small piece of yellow paper. He took the microphone in hand and said, "Our group number one is the "Selke and Montana Families!" Two small families near us cheered. "I doubt we'll even get chosen," I told Syleria Susae. "The probability of our paper in the bucket getting drawn is 1 in 62," she continued to predict in mathematical form. "Thanks for telling me," I groaned. Just then the manager announced the second grand prize group, "Marie Roberts and Suzanne Leopard!" Groups of teenagers started screaming and cheering and chanting Marie Roberts and Suzanne Leopard's names.

"I know we'll be the third group," Mr. Louis quietly predicted. "How can you be so sure of that?" I asked. "Our piece of paper is slightly larger than everyone else because we had to fit all of our names on it. So we may have an 85% chance at least," he predicted.

"And now for our last group of winners . . . The Dream Detective Dogs Club!" the manager lastly announced. At that point, I couldn't believe my ears. Had he really announced the name of our team? For a few seconds, my friends had frozen in surprise, but now they were hopping up and down barking and yapping! When a couple of minutes had passed, I started doing the same like my friends, happy and excited with delight. The truth is dogs can't help staying calm all the time. We just have to let out our excitement. When the crowd started to disappear and diminish, the manager gave us tips and instructions about super sleuthing. "Remember, this is a dangerous crime we're talking about. This robber has probably left some clues behind. I would be glad to investigate, but I have significant work and papers to catch up on and I would contact the Feline & K9 Companions, but they're on vacation and out of reach so I don't have much of a choice," said the manager with a heavy sigh. I knew exactly how he felt. I also wished that the modern sleuths, Feline & K9 Companions would solve the case. They were more experienced detectives.

Lastly the manager gave us a quick tour of the part of the exhibit we would be investigating. It wasn't much of a tour without the main attraction: the gemstones. As I was passing a display stand, I spotted a pink bracelet with red diamond shaped jewels. For some reason, it seemed vaguely familiar. Did I see something like this before? Wait a minute! I tried to remember what had happened earlier today. Was there something related between the bracelet and the crime we had to solve? I wasn't sure. Could it be a clue? "Allie Angie, do you remember seeing that bracelet, before?" I asked her. "No, but it's probably just a missing piece of jewelry someone dropped. I don't think it means anything special," she replied. That remark made me feel more suspicious about the bracelet. But why would someone's bracelet be left on the ruby display stand? It just didn't make any sense. I remembered that it looked just like the bracelet Marie Roberts was wearing earlier and showing off to the rest of the rest of the teenagers. I quickly took a glance at Marie Roberts who was in the exhibit too, but had not noticed the bracelet. On her left arm was a pink bracelet with red jewels. Yep they definitely had to be the same. I picked up the bracelet on the floor and tied it on my collar. At least I wouldn't lose it.

If Marie Roberts had two of the same bracelets, how could this one have gotten near a display stand? The empty ruby display stands were farther away than the closest gemstone stands near the entrance of the exhibit. It was actually near the wall on the other side of the room where the rubies belong. But yesterday the display stands near the walls were blocked off with plastic orange cones due to the unexpected robbery. Then how could Marie Roberts have gotten past the cones without anyone noticing? It seemed awfully strange.

Later that evening back at home, I scheduled a meeting with the whole club. We all gathered in the living room on the coffee table. The table is actually pretty long and almost fills up the room's space. We use it as a counsel center. Because the table is rectangular Syleria Susae sits at one end and I sit at the other end with three dogs per side of the table.

Tonight Mr. and Mrs. Louis had gone out to dinner. But they knew we could take care of ourselves in the meantime. I explained what I saw to the rest of the club. All but one didn't think Marie Roberts was a suspect (And that one was me!).

"I think you've gone a little off with your investigation, Mario Marco," remarked Delilah Mara. She obviously had her secret notebook out and was probably writing down more stuff as she usually does. "But-," I started to say but was interrupted. "I agree too. I mean, there is not really a chance that she could have stolen anything. I mean, how could a teenage girl steal something so valuable?" asked Syleria Susae intently. But Allie Angie asked a question that made me nervous all over, "Do you have any evidence, proof, or clues that Marie Roberts did anything?" "I found her bracelet near the rubies display stand," I answered as I raised the bracelet high for everyone to see. "True, but I think we need more than that to better clear up what REALLY happened," Delilah Mara stated. Everyone else agreed with her. That was unusually strange because hardly anyone pays attention to Delilah Mara. "Everyone, I think she just might be the ultimate robber," I declared, "And even if you don't agree with me, I'll find proof one way or another." I quickly ran off. If they weren't going to believe me, I would just handle this mystery on my own without them.

That night, before I went to bed, I took Delilah Mara's notebook and a flashlight to the living room while everyone was asleep. I crawled under a small table and switched on the flashlight. (It actually belonged to Syleria Susae.) Then I flipped open to the page Delilah Mara had left off on and had currently written in so far. (So far she had used 18 pages.) This time, I was surprised at what I saw. There were things about everyone on almost every page:

GABRIEL GORDON HAS A WHITE HAIR ON HIS BACK. I WONDER IF HE IS GETTING OLD ALREADY.

That didn't seem too unusual because Gabriel Gordon's family line included both black and WHITE poodles.

ROYAL ROMEO DOES NOT HAVE ANY MONEY IN HIS PIGGY BANK. IF HIS NAME REALLY MEANS HE IS ROYAL, WHY DOESN'T HE HAVE ANY MONEY?

ALLIE ANGIE'S PIMPLE OR WART IS A
REALLY A MOSQUITO BITE. IF SHE
DOESN'T DO ANYTHING ABOUT IT,
SHE'LL BE SCRATCHING AND ITCHING
IT UNTIL IT BLEEDS. THAT JUST
MIGHT ATRACT MORE MOSQUITOES.

I obviously didn't think
mosquitoes were a big problem.
Because I am a poodle, I have
thick and curly fur. With all this
fluff, you wouldn't even be a
close target for those measly
bugs.

PIERRE STINKS LIKE DUST, WORMS,
AND GARBAGE! IF I WERE MRS. LOUIS,
I WOULD TAKE HIM MORE BATHS. WE
CAN'T HAVE A CLUB WITH SMELLY
DOGS. THEN EVERYONE WILL THINK
WE'RE CONTAGIOUS! WE NEED HELP!
FREQUENTLY!

SYLERIA SUSAE BETTER DO A GOOD JOB
AS PRESIDENT, OR ELSE I'LL
NOMINATE MYSELF FOR BEING A MORE
SUITABLE LEADER AND TO LEAD A MORE
RESPONSIBLE CLUB.

VANESSA PANA'S PINK FUR IS GETTING
OUT OF HAND. IF IT KEEPS ON
GROWING LIGHTER SHE'LL LOOK MORE

LIKE "VANESSA PANA THE FLAMINGO COLORED CLOWN." WHAT A HUGE DISGRACE!!!

MARIO MARCO HAS TOO MANY BOOKS. 5 POETRY, 3 FOLKTALE, 8 DRAMA, 6 SCIENCE AND PHYSICS, 4 ROMANCE, 10 MYSTERY AND CRIME. IF HE DOESN'T WATCH OUT, HE WILL BECOME SO OBSESSED, HE'LL END UP MAKING MORE THAN ENOUGH MISTAKES WHILE SOLVING REAL MYSTERIES THAN THOSE FICTION ONES IN THOSE BORING NOVELS.

Now that made me so mad that I could have ripped up Delilah Mara's notebook in half, and maybe in a million pieces! But I didn't since the whole club would have thought I would have gone quack in seconds! I guess Miss Mara has her ways. But she doesn't know that not all my mystery and crime books are fiction. I decided to get some rest. I'm gonna solve this mystery and I will start as soon as possible. Possible it would be tomorrow! It was time to show the club that I could be an experienced sleuth too. I knew that Marie Roberts had to be the gemstone thief. Who else?

Chapter 4: The Three Chosen Groups and a Lost Bracelet

I returned Syleria Susae's flashlight and the notebook to Delilah Mara. The truth was, I didn't feel like giving these things back, but if I didn't, the club members might kick me out of the group if they wanted to. That, I wouldn't be able to stand.

Chapter 5: Marie Roberts AKA Current Suspect

July 25th, Monday - 12:30 p.m.

Delilah Mara - I'm not so sure about your intelligence on this one, Mario Marco.

Mario Marco - Delilu Marra, tooday haf of us r going too spie on Marie Roberts while the rest of us investigat the igsibit.

Delilah Mara - You mean "exhibit," Mario Marco. Also, I'm not so sure that your suspect's puny bracelet will give us any clues or results. To me, it seems suspicious how you can spell Marie Roberts's name, but not mine!

Syleria Susae - Stop fighting! If Mario Marco is wrong, we shouldn't yell at him too much. He's trying his best to help us out. I think only four of us should go to the museum today with Mr. Louis. We don't want so many dogs in one place, you know.

Chapter 5: Marie Roberts AKA Current Suspect

Delilah Mara - If Mario Marco is going, I hope he'll solve this crime correctly like an experienced detective. If not, then I will nominate myself as the new vice president of the club. I'll take my secret notebook and tell you any comments about Mario Marco, Syleria Susae.

Mario Marco - Hey! U cant do that! Being vise presidint is my jobb!

Delilah Mara - The truth is, Mario Marco, the vice president is supposed to be smart and always right. On my point, you make an extremely bad speller!

Syleria Susae - Quit fighting, Delilah Mara or else we'll never start investigating.

Mario Marco - Yeah, Miss Mara of the Mocking.

Syleria Susae - Our day started with a trip to a "half empty" exhibit. We didn't find much, but Mario Marco's suspect is beginning to seem a little bit suspicious.

Chapter 5: Marie Roberts AKA Current Suspect

At 9:23 a.m, Mrs. Louis took Delilah Mara, Syleria Susae, Allie Angie, and I to the museum for our first day on the job. Marie Roberts and Suzanne Leopard, plus the other detective groups were already there. I think they're early on purpose. Delilah Mara and Syleria Susae would be looking among the rubies, diamonds, and emeralds. Mr. Louis promised to provide them with assistance if needed. "I hope you're sure about this," whispered Allie Angie. "Don't worry about this case, Allie Angie. We're only doing a little bit of spying and detective work. Hopefully we may find more evidence that Marie Roberts is a true suspect," I replied with a positive grin.

As I sneaked quietly with Allie Angie, she took out a small notepad and pencil. At that point, we saw Marie Roberts chatting away with her friend, Suzanne Leopard. "I wonder what would happen if we solve the mystery and earn money!" wondered Suzanne. "At least I might be able to owe Gracie money she demanded in replacement of the cat she stole once. But too bad I need to pay her in jewelry. I already had two pure ruby bracelets and I was going to give her one, but I lost one of them. Now what will I be able to do?" asked Marie Roberts helplessly. "Those jewels on your bracelet are pure rubies. You could give her the one you're wearing now," suggested Suzanne Leopard. "But the rubies on this bracelet don't belong to me," complained Marie Roberts. "What do you mean?" asked Suzanne Leopard with a very puzzled expression. Marie Roberts whispered something to her in a low voice. After that, Allie Angie and I went to a corner of the exhibit.

"She does seem suspicious," commented Allie Angie. "Now do you believe me?" I exploded. "Absolutely! Look, I took notes," replied Allie Angie. She held up her notepad and showed me what she wrote. My eyes widened and I awed, "You wrote all of this in 5 minutes?" "Well actually, I am a fast writer," said Allie Angie.

The first few pages had a short summary of some suspects:

MARIE ROBERTS

AGE: 15
Grade: 9th
Hair: curly, short and brown.
Other: She owes jewelry to Gracie for replacement of a stolen cat that she catnapped and later lost. Might involve something with the bracelet Mario Marco found.

VANESSA MCATEE

A lady with long black hair that reaches past her back. The thief who stole the meteorites the first time. The Feline & K9 Companions were solving the case then.

GRACIE MCCARTHY

A circus performer who catnapped one of members from the Feline & K9 Companions.

"Let's go tell Syleria Susae and Delilah Mara!" I exclaimed. We ran back and told our friends. Syleria Susae and Delilah Mara seemed really surprised when we told them what Marie Roberts and

Suzanne Leopard had discussed. "Sorry if we didn't believe you," Syleria Susae apologized sadly. I forgave Syleria Susae and Allie Angie. "Well I don't care! Marie Roberts probably isn't our prime suspect, anyway!" snapped Delilah Mara. She opened her notebook and snatched Allie Angie's pen. I knew she was going to write more stuff:

IF MARIO MARCO KEEPS ON LOOKING AT ME IN THAT WISHY WASHY WAY, I'LL GIVE HIS FACE A SATISFYING PUNCH.

Delilah Mara walked away and the rest of us stared at her with shocked faces. We were too speechless to say anything. "If Delilah Mara won't believe us, we'll go after Marie Roberts ourselves," announced Syleria Susae defiantly. Usually she is a very quiet puppy. "We'll think and try to find ways to prove that Marie Roberts is a suspect," said Allie Angie.

That evening, back at home, Syleria Susae called for a meeting in her bedroom. "We have three suspects: Marie Roberts, Vanessa

McAtee, or Gracie McCarthy," she said. When our counsel began, I, Mario Marco, stood up in front of everyone.

"Marie Roberts just might be our thief because she owes jewelry to her boss named Gracie McCarthy. Gracie McCarthy wants jewels in exchange of one of the Feline and K9 Companion cats that she stole and lost," I explained. "That sounds vaguely familiar," suspected Delilah Mara.

Then Delilah Mara started to explain, "My cousin, Jackson said he knew of a skillful circus performer, Gracie McCarthy, who signed up as a detective for the museum when the gemstones were stolen the very first time last month. Gracie McCarthy really wanted a popular cat from the Feline & K9 Companions. So she stole Patience, an intelligent Siamese cat, from her owner, Sophie LeLaine. The canine Jackson and the other cat members had to rescue her. After Gracie McCarthy and a friend Julia were in jail, her heart had a craving for money."

Everyone stared at Delilah Mara with astonished expressions. "I was just trying to help," she muttered. Pierre decided to put in more information to break up the silence, "Vanessa McAtee was the lady who stole the meteorites. Her husband is out of jail and runs their museum, The Sacramento Adventure. She wanted the meteorites so she could display them as an attraction for their museum. But the gemstone thief was an employee of the museum named Griffin Randolph. He's still in jail."

And again that brought more silence. "Look everybody! We have clues and suspects, but no answers. I suggest that some of us should spy on Marie Roberts again. Are any of you with me?" I asked out loud. The whole club cheered and chanted (including Delilah Mara). That night, I glanced through her notebook:

MARIE ROBERTS LOOKS LIKE A MUTANT
SHEEP OF A PERSON WITH TOO TIGHT
OF CURLS ON HER HEAD.

I SAW ROYAL ROMEO WHEN NOBODY WAS
LOOKING AND HE WAS PICKING WAX OUT
OF HIS EARS. IT WAS DISGUSTING!
THE WAX WAS BROWN. EW!!

That was much better. You
see, the way the notebook reading
system works is that you want to
act correct and positive at all
times. In our household, Delilah
Mara is like a magazine composer
and she sure does like writing and
spreading rumors. But the main
warning is, no one wants their
name in her notebook. Your goal
would be trying not to find your
name on every page. If you lived
with Delilah Mara, you might
become insane for your sanity. But
she still is a great friend. Her
bad temper is what you may want to
avoid. When things don't go her
way, well I guess she might as
well understand for once that
she's not always right.

Chapter 6: The Unusual Suspicion

It was July 27th. The festival was approaching and was only a few days away. Our main trouble was that we still had not found out anything else. We currently had one of Marie Roberts's ruby bracelets, but that didn't lead us anywhere else than tell us that Marie Roberts was a suspect. We cleared up more information at 3:27 p.m.

Mr. Louis took Allie Angie, Vanessa Pana, Delilah Mara, and Syleria Susae to the museum's exhibit for another lengthy investigation. It was unfortunate I couldn't go since I was really looking forward to another visit. As Syleria Susae and Delilah Mara were searching for clues among the display stands, Vanessa Pana and Allie Angie snuck up near Marie Roberts to hear more of her mysterious conversations.

Part II: Allie Angie

Good afternoon visitor, it's Allie Angie here telling the story. I'll let you know how our eavesdropping situation went. As I was riding in the car, on the way over to the museum earlier, I had stared out the window for a few moments deep in thought. For some reason this crime didn't seem to be giving much clues. For one, we had no idea who might have stolen the gemstones. And the only option we could do was to take chances and guess who did it. I recognize I know this was definitely not a very wise decision for a group of sleuths. Well, what did the world expect us to be? Experienced detectives or what?

Then something had occurred to me. What if Gracie McCarthy or what if Vanessa McAtee were out of jail somehow? It could be possible. Marie Roberts might also be a thief too. Even though she may just be an ordinary teenager, who knows what she might be planning to do in the future? Also, what if it was someone else?

Chapter 6: The Unusual Suspicion

Maybe someone else we hadn't expected? Oh, everything was so totally confusing! "We're here!" Vanessa Pana had cheered. I awoke from my thoughts and saw that everyone was getting out of the car. I hopped out the backseat and in the parking lot.

As I entered the museum, I spotted the two other detective groups. They were on their way to the top floor. We went up the stairs to the exhibit. "I hope Mario Marco's suggestion really works. I'm no Harriet the Spy," Syleria Susae had complained to me. She didn't look too happy about what we were about to do. "Don't worry, Vanessa Pana and I will do the spying for you guys," I reassured her with a comforting smile.

I got my notepad where I had taken notes a couple of days ago. When we had opened the doors of the exhibit, Syleria Susae and Delilah Mara would be looking for more clues around the "Ruby Section." As Vanessa Pana and I went behind a counter near Marie

Roberts, I was surprised to hear
her talking to a lovely looking
blond haired girl of the same age,
Jane. Vanessa Pana and I lifted
our ears to listen better.

"I can't give up my bracelet,
Jane. I used to have two, but I
lost one. So I am keeping this one
for myself," said Marie Roberts.
"If you still want to keep your
job in the circus, give those
jewels to me and I will hand them
over to my boss, Gracie McCarthy.
Gracie McCarthy, our circus
performer, needs them to pay her
fine to get out of jail!" yelled
Jane. "No way, that would be like
cheating and double stealing!
Those jewels will make me rich so
I can retire from being an animal
trainer and become a world
renowned explorer," replied Marie
Roberts. "You said you had more
jewels. Where are they? You could
at least give Gracie McCarthy two
or three!" grumbled Jane. "I
won't!" snapped Marie Roberts.
"Where did you hide the key to
your secret hiding place?"
demanded Jane. "Why should I tell
you? You don't even know where my

hiding place is!" screamed Marie Roberts. "Just give me a hint," pleaded Jane.

"Look for something full of hay, dressed like a human, and despised by birds. Use the key you find inside and find an area where fossils are cleaned, tested, and are prepared for display. The key is not here, but it is in a building south from here. Gracie McCarthy's friend knows a lot about this place," finished Marie Roberts as she stormed off and walked away and headed toward her friend, Suzanne Leopard.

"Whoa, this is more than frequent!" gasped Vanessa Pana. I glanced at the notes I had written on my notepad:

"LOOK FOR SOMETHING FULL OF HAY, DRESSED LIKE A HUMAN, AND DESPISED BY BIRDS. THE KEY IS INSIDE AND GO TO A PLACE WHERE FOSSILS ARE PREPARED FOR GOING OUT ON DISPLAY. THE KEY IS SOUTH IN A BUILDING WHERE GRACIE MCCARTHY'S FRIEND KNOWS A LOT ABOUT."

I read the last statement and my eyes widened. "You didn't really think that circus performer, Gracie McCarthy, had anything to do with this case, did you?" asked Vanessa Pana. "Wow. I never thought that she could have been so revengeful," I quietly answered. "Tell me about it," moaned Vanessa Pana.

The reality was, I wasn't expecting a catnapper to be a jewel thief. I wondered how Mario Marco and everyone else were doing at home. When Vanessa Pana and I told everything about our findings to Syleria Susae and Delilah Mara, they were completely speechless. Delilah Mara had brought her secret notebook again and was busily writing in it:

I'M SO SORRY IF I DIDN'T BELIEVE YOU, MARIO MARCO. BUT I THINK MARIE ROBERTS REALLY MIGHT HAVE SOMETHING TO DO WITH THIS CASE. I STILL CONSIDER MARIE ROBERTS TO LOOK LIKE A MUTANT SHEEP. (I DIDN'T KNOW SHEEP HAD SUCH BAD TEMPERS.) MARIE ROBERTS'S FRIEND, SUZANNE LEOPARD LOOKS LIKE A

GOLDEN RETRIEVER WITH FAT FLUFFY
FUR.

THAT GIRL, JANE SURE NEEDS A MAKE-
OVER. SHE ALMOST LOOKS LIKE GRACIE
MCCARTHY HERSELF. HER SKIN IS
DEADLY WHITE AND HER HAIR IS
WHITISH YELLOW. IF SHE AND GRACIE
MCCARTHY ARE RELATED, THEY ARE
PROBABLY ALIENS WHO HAVE COME TO
INVADE THE WORLD. (NASA, WE ARE
UNDER ATTACK!!!)

It's funny how Delilah Mara
loves carrying that notebook
around, I thought.

Part III: Royal Romeo

As Allie Angie, Syleria
Susae, Vanessa Pana, and Delilah
Mara went to the museum for their
spying investigation, the rest of
us, (Mario Marco, Gabriel Gordon,
Pierre, and I) stayed home.
Gabriel Gordon and I were watching
the news while Pierre and Mario
Marco were reading comic books
upstairs. They were borrowing
books of "Calvin and Hobbes" and
"Garfield," which were ones I
purchased at a book fair.

Chapter 6: The Unusual Suspicion

On TV, were updates on sports, news, and entertainment. New movies like Ice Age 2: The Meltdown, Cars, and The Wild would be coming out on DVD and VHS pretty soon! The entertainment previews were mostly about the lives of Kelly Clarkson, Angelina Jolie, and more Hollywood stars. That was extremely boring. I think what really interested me was the news. There was more war in this country called Iraq, a satellite was recently sent to Pluto several months ago for research, and an update was announced on our county's museum! Well, it didn't really mention anything about the museum; it was just an interview of the detective groups.

Mr. Louis was the one who was seen on TV the most. After we watched the interview, we went to the kitchen to eat an afternoon snack. The neat thing about Mrs. Louis is that she is a very well organized person. She just loves keeping things in a specific order. Her dresser drawer and her wardrobe are large in height because of her organization of fabrics. For example, the socks have their own set of drawers according to their colors. I know, it's seems really weird, but I guess Mrs. Louis intends to keep it that way. Because everything is put in so orderly, we can't open a cupboard, closet, or door without finding everything labeled and put in place. If you saw our kitchen, you would go nuts over the pantry, especially. The pantry is divided into two. One side of the pantry belongs to us and the other side is for our owners.

On the "canine" side, you'll find bones, dog treats, canned foods, steak, chicken, beef, and a little bit of fish. Yuck! I don't know why Mario Marco likes tuna so much! We all formed a straight line in front of the pantry door and one by one got our snacks individually. Gabriel Gordon got beef and I decided on a fresh chicken leg. Mario Marco received his tuna and gobbled it up messily in the kitchen as soon as he got the can open a crack. I couldn't stand the smell, so I hurried out of the kitchen to another room:

the living room. Pierre is more on the neat side as he picked up a mini bag of dog veggies and biscuits. Lately he has been trying to stick to a more efficient and successful diet. Gabriel Gordon joined in on the comic books while I settled down to a newspaper on the coffee table.

Nowadays, ever since the robbery, I haven't been reading much of my comic and joke books. So for the past several days, I changed my reading strategy to world news and U.S. entertainment. If you asked me, there are very few dogs I know who have been interested in getting a Hollywood career. The only famous dogs that are quite known in our perspective of entertainment would be Lassie and Air Bud, a collie and golden retriever of the 1990's.

What's surprised me is that Mario Marco and Pierre have tried imitating my humor, but lately had not luck. I just recently lent them seven comic books and a magazine titled, "How to Be a Living Comedy."

As I opened the newspaper, I skimmed through the pages. During the first couple of minutes, I spotted no articles that would lead me to further interest. Some of those boring articles were, "Late 4th of July Fireworks On Sale," "Early Labor Day in San Diego," "Sheryl Crow's Late Tour in Eastern U.S;" "Jesse McCartney's new album: Right Where You Want Me," and "Traffic Confusion in Los Angeles."

I groaned and looked at the newspaper's table of contents. "Either nothing much is going on this week or maybe they need better interviewers to conduct the California Gazette," I thought. The table of contents is worth looking than wasting your time looking through the whole thing. Our weekly paper is usually 20 pages long. But it contains nothing in the new but advertisements with some of the worst deals you could get. Just as I was about to finish looking down the table of contents I saw in gigantic letters:

ADMINISTRATOR ESCAPES JAIL - P. 12

I quickly flipped to the reported page and there in capitalized letters and big exclamation points read:

ADMINISTRATOR VANESSA MCATEE ESCAPES FROM PRISON!!!!!!!!!!

I read the entire article and then called Mario Marco, Pierre, and Gabriel Gordon. After they read the page, we stared at the words for a few moments. I just couldn't believe what I had just read. "Um, guys I hate to admit it, but I think Vanessa McAtee is out of jail," I announced. Mario Marco turned the page and on the other side was a photo of Vanessa McAtee herself!

On top of the picture in big bright red letters was the word: MISSING! At the bottom of the picture were Vanessa McAtee's age, height, weight, day of birth, hair color, eye color, and skin color, plus the day she was last seen which was July 23rd. Wow this hadn't been new. Vanessa McAtee had been missing for a few days now. "I think we should focus on Vanessa McAtee and Marie Roberts. They both seem to be extra suspicious," said Gabriel Gordon. "Yeah, we might as well forget about Gracie McCarthy anyway. She can't do anything because she's still in jail," muttered Mario Marco.

This sudden news seemed to hit us like lightening. It was strange how so much could have happened over a period of several days. What will occur next? I didn't know, but I sure didn't want to find out.

Chapter 7: The Meteorites are Missing!

Today was totally shocking. I, **Royal Romeo**, hate to admit it, but it really did seem that way. We had never known all this time that Vanessa McAtee had been so determined that she found a way to escape from jail. That evening, Allie Angie, Vanessa Pana, Delilah Mara, and Syleria Susae, came home and were grieved when it came time to tell our story.

"I just can't believe she could have been behind all this," sighed Allie Angie and Vanessa Pana. "I told you that Marie Roberts didn't have anything to do with our crime," remarked Delilah Mara. "Wait just a minute, Delilah! One person may not have caused all this trouble. Think like a detective for once, anyway. When solving a mystery, look for the facts and don't jump to conclusions," I declared thoughtfully. "That's really practical advice," Pierre complimented. "Where did you find that out?" asked Delilah Mara intently. "From one of Mario Marco's mystery books of course. What do you think?" I snapped. By the look on her face, I could tell that Delilah Mara seemed extremely beat and disgusted.

While I discussed more on how to be a better sleuth, from the corner of my eye, I saw Allie Angie pick up the newspaper and study it carefully. It seemed like a long time until she finally placed it back on its original place which was the coffee table in our living room. Pierre had timed it and said she stared without blinking for almost 7 minutes! Wow! Another world record! It seemed like things were increasing in high ranks in the category of competition as I would call it. But I think we shouldn't talk so much about all this distraction. Sleuths never get distracted, so we'll get back to our first subject.

At 7:00 p.m., Mr. Louis arrived home from work. We were all seated at the dining room table having supper at the time. Dinner, as I sometimes call it seemed unusually boring that night. USUALLY we joke, laugh, and talk about fun activities we plan later in the week. But what we were experiencing now was not funny as you can read. Well, duh. A mystery in truth is normally not fun at all to solve. You get confused, scared, angry, depressed, and worst of all, kicked off by your peers at times especially if they don't see a suspect as important as you do. Mario Marco and Delilah Mara's situation with Marie Roberts is one of my fewest examples.

Back to dinner, I suppose. At the dinner table, there was hardly any movement. We ate our food in almost total silence which makes me feel uncomfortable. When it comes to times like this, we only eat like a crumb of our food and spend the rest of the next half hour just staring at everyone's blank facial expressions beside or from across the table. I know; it really is a dull way to pass the time. The food seemed to sit squishy and soggy on our plates. If you didn't know, Mrs. Louis had fixed us some salty mashed potatoes and lamb chops which was a couple of days old before the expiration date. For desert, Mr. and Mrs. Louis ate cereal and toast while the rest of us dogs were stuck snacking on leftover tuna.

Everyone seemed so sad and lonely. Mr. Louis wore clothes of gray and black colours and Mrs. Louis was dressed in a variety of cold colors ranging from dark olive green to an almost pitch black plum purple. When it came time to go to bed, we turned out the lights one by one in quietness.

As I slept, I wondered what could be happening. "How could this be possible? Could I be dreaming?" I thought. I stayed up for most of the night just staring out the window at the moon which was blocked by a few ghostly looking clouds. I quickly turned away. If I keep this up, I'll scare my mind to death and even worse, haunt myself. My head was just about to lay on my pillow when I heard a faint echoing siren.

Quietly, I crept to the nearest window sill and peered out in the night and darkness. The neighborhood seemed all nice and sound asleep except for one thing. Down the street were red and blue lights. I leaned my ear against the window to listen more clearly and therefore I did hear the echoing wailing of sirens. "That only means one thing! The museum may be in trouble!" I gasped. Very quickly and quietly, I went over to wake up Gabriel Gordon. He immediately sat up in his bed and probably didn't recognize me at first because he started yelping, "Ahh! Help! Our home has been invaded by aliens! Aliens, everyone! It's the beginning of the War of the Worlds!" I covered his mouth and told him it was me, Royal Romeo. He was quickly relieved and he revealed to me how he had a dream about blood sucking aliens. Well, he did read a comic book about aliens earlier, so no wonder he had those thoughts in his mind 24 hours straight.

I told Gabriel Gordon about the sirens I just heard. "That sounds unusual, indeed. Do you think we should follow them and see where they're heading?" he asked worriedly. "That's exactly what I was about to suggest," I replied and added, "Let's take this camera. It could be of further need." I spotted a small camera laying on a table beside my bed. As Gabriel Gordon looked for a bag to put the camera in, I could hear the sirens coming closer and closer. I was surprised that nobody else in the house or even in the neighborhood woke up. "Heavy sleepers just ruin everything in a time of trouble," I thought.

When Gabriel Gordon found a bag, I decided to carry it over my neck and went downstairs to the first floor. Gabriel Gordon followed me saying, "I just know it's the police." We raced out the doggie door in the front door, down a staircase, and out the apartment lobby. Just as we went down the main door at the front of the apartment, three police cars passed by. It took great effort, but we caught up with their cars and followed them to their destination which actually happened to be the museum! "Something must be terribly wrong!" whimpered Gabriel Gordon. "Who knows? Maybe another robbery?" I asked. "At 10:40 p.m.? I don't think so," he replied.

If you didn't know, it really took probably more GREAT effort to get to the museum. We had to be careful not to be seen and be cautious when going on roads or crossing streets. To tell you something, Gabriel Gordon almost got run over by an SUV. "We should protest!" he teasingly declared as we were safe in hiding. At one point, we had almost lost sight of the police cars. So you see, mystery solving IS a lot harder than it seems.

"It could be a robbery. If so, I think it has something to do with our suspects," I finished. We had spoken no more until we had reached the museum. It had been flooded with police, security guards, employees, the museum manager, plus news interviewers with cameras.

"What's going on?" asked a lady. "It seems to be that our meteorites have been stolen and the whole exhibit has been robbed!" replied the museum manager sadly. "That's strange, though. How could a robbery have occurred at this time of night?" asked a man from the employee crowd. "We are trying to find that out," informed a police officer. The conversation continued and while that went on, I heard a slight rustling noise.

"Do you hear something?" I asked. "I think so," whispered Gabriel Gordon and added, "Where do you think it's coming from?" I sniffed the air and caught a strange scent. "Follow me," I commanded. I smelled the scent and it led me to the side of the museum. "Are you sure you know where you're going?" wondered

Gabriel Gordon. "I think so. By the way, what are we following?" I questioned. "Beats me, Royal Romeo. But I think that's a question you should ask yourself," Gabriel Gordon corrected me. Up ahead were trees, bushes, and flowers.

All of a sudden, a huge gust of wind slapped against our faces, which made shivers go down my spine. The trees and bushes were hit with the wind and they started to make constant loud rustling noises. Unusually I noticed that one of the bushes was rustling a lot louder than the others. "You must have mistaken the wind for that noise. I'm sure it's nothing," Gabriel Gordon corrected me again. "Wait a minute, Gabriel Gordon. Before we reach a final conclusion, we must see what is behind this bush in particular," I suggested. We quietly snuck behind a small tree near the bush. As soon as we saw what was behind the bush, we were surprised to see two hideous looking figures!

Chapter 7: The Meteorites are Missing!

They were kneeling before each other examining some objects from a few bags they had laid on the ground. We eased our ears to hear in on their conversation.

"I have finally inherited this fabulous fortune. The meteorites at last! Now, I shall add them to my exhibit collection and my museum shall be almost complete!" exclaimed a female voice. Oh no! These must be the thieves who stole the meteorites! "Pretty soon, we'll get even with Marie Roberts and make her tell us where the key to the gemstones are. We'll split the amount of gemstones and share it between you and my aunt," replied a familiar voice. It was the voice of the girl who had spoken with Marie Roberts! "Good thinking, Jessica! At 4:00 a.m., we'll be on our way to San Francisco. Miss Vanessa McAtee shall strike once again!" the first figure cackled with an evil accent.

As Jessica and her partner got up and gathered their valuables, I shot several pictures of them with my camera. The two robbers eventually headed to their nearby vehicle which was a bright red SUV.

"This is terrible! Not only do we know who stole the meteorites and gemstones, but now they're going to be placed in a region out of our reach! Also, that was probably Vanessa McAtee! She's got the meteorites and eventually she really will get the gemstones! What are we going to do?" I moaned.

"Tomorrow, we'll try to persuade our owners to take us to the Sacramento Adventure. It's our only choice," Gabriel Gordon concluded. He was right. If we had to save the meteorites, this would be the time to take risks!

Chapter 8: Faraway Destination

Part IV: Allie Angie

It was July 26th. I just couldn't believe it! From the perspective of Royal Romeo and Gabriel Gordon, that must have been a risk to see the thieves up close. Mr. and Mrs. Louis were quite shocked. "You could have been hurt! I don't want you to be outside at night near dangerous people without adult supervision from adults," they had warned the two adventurous puppies.

At breakfast, Royal Romeo and Gabriel Gordon had mentioned the Sacramento Adventure. "We'll have to think about that," said Mr. Louis thoughtfully. "But they have the meteorites. At 4:00 a.m., they would be on their way to Sacramento already!" exclaimed Gabriel Gordon. "Please! We could actually save our county!" begged Syleria Susae, Pierre, and Mario Marco altogether. They sounded like a chorus of sad dogs singing on minor scales. "I guess we

could. We might as well be on our
way to the Sacramento Adventure.
I'll start getting ready at noon.
But remember, I am not planning to
rent a hotel or stay for a couple
of weeks," promised Mr. Louis.

"Yea!" we all cheered. "But
only three of you may go. I don't
want too many dogs in a public
place!" he finished. We were all
happy that we were going to solve
the mystery, but we were
disappointed since not all of us
could go. That led to more
fighting between Delilah Mara and
Mario Marco. It was when we were
choosing our three lucky
detectives.

"Allow me to go. I'm the one
who persuaded the club to uncover
this crime," announced Mario
Marco. "Oh no, you don't! You
might make a mistake!" commented
Delilah Mara. To stop the
fighting, I went right up and
said, "You know what? I've got a
deal to make with you guys."
Delilah Mara and Mario Marco look
over at me and curiously asked,
"WHAT?"

"Why don't you both stay and we'll find someone else other than you two. That way there will be no arguing," I stated. Delilah Mara and Mario Marco looked at each other for a moment and I walked away. "You know, that sounds like a great idea," agreed Mario Marco. "Yep, it sure does," added Delilah Mara. But frowns of confusion spread across their faces and they both complained, "Wait a minute, what did you say again, Allie Angie?" It was too late. I had already walked off.

"I have an idea! Let's draw names out of a cup and those top three names that are first picked will be the lucky winners of our traveling detectives giveaway!" Pierre suggested. Syleria Susae gave to the idea and wrote everyone's names on separate little pieces of paper (Except for Mario Marco and Delilah Mara's). At 11:00 a.m. sharp, we gathered around the living room table. It was time to draw the three lucky names. "I hope I get picked!" squealed Syleria Susae. "Me too," hoped Vanessa Pana and Pierre.

"Everyone, settle down! Mrs. Louis will draw the winners in a few minutes!" I announced out loud. Approximately 4 minutes later, Mrs. Louis came and sat on the couch with the cup in her hand.

Without looking she slowly drew out three folded pieces of paper and said aloud, "Our three detectives are Royal Romeo, Allie Angie, and Vanessa Pana"!

In our little crowd were shouts, barks, smiles, groans, and cheering all at the same time! Syleria Susae and Gabriel Gordon looked extremely displeased. Vanessa Pana and I were jumping up and down with excitement. At 11:40 a.m., Vanessa Pana, Royal Romeo, and I piled up in Mrs. Louis's jet black colored car. Vanessa Pana was listening to music on a pair of headphones and on an MP3 player while Royal Romeo discussed another matter with Mr. Louis. They had been talking about the photos he and Gabriel Gordon had taken during the night of the meteorites' robbery. "You are an extremely intelligent sleuth,

Royal Romeo. I think these pictures just might come in handy," Mr. Louis praised. He was actually sort of proud that we had more clues. Lately the news reporters that had interviewed us recently were getting kind of bored since we had no information or updates to tell them. Well, guess what? Our luck turned up for once!

"Let me see those pictures, Royal Romeo," I said. As I scanned through seven photos I exclaimed in curiosity, "How did you capture these images without the thieves seeing you? The camera's flash is usually bright and makes lots of sound. How did you do it?" I was so eager to know how Royal Romeo and Gabriel Gordon could have gotten so close to take these. "It took some time to figure out, but I was able to turn the flash off. By the way, it was a pretty windy night. The rustling of the trees and bushes practically blocked out the sound," he answered thoughtfully.

The first picture was of the two robbers holding the meteorites. The next was what I would recall interesting. I caught the sight of their faces and expressions and the third photo was a snap-shot of the thieves' red SUV. Then I knew I got this all figured out! "This will be easy! All we need to do is find a red SUV with two robbers!" I stated. "I'm not so sure about that, Allie Angie. In the entire state and throughout the country, there are hundreds of vehicles with very close and maybe even matching descriptions. The only way we'll tell them apart is by looking at the license plate and studying the numbers on the back of each car," added Mr. Louis. "Oh," I sighed in disappointment. I guess this won't be as easy as I thought. I think Mr. Louis could tell I was feeling discouraged because he recalled, "But don't give up just yet. We may see Jessica and Vanessa McAtee. Even though, this may not be a walk-through-the-doggy-door-task, you may want to know that we're not dealing with any ordinary people, but dangerous robbers." "Royal Romeo, you may want to find more photos of that SUV. Hopefully, there might be another photo of their vehicle," I suggested. Royal Romeo carefully flipped through every page of his museum robbery photo collection. In the end, he found three shots of the mystery vehicle.

"There's one of the front, one of the side, and another of the back of the SUV," he announced. "Let's take a look at the last one," I decided. We both studied the photo. It was sort of blurry, but at least the license plate was readable. The numbers and letters seemed really small. "Oh bother, now what shall we do?" I moaned. "I brought a bag and I think it has a magnifying glass," said Vanessa Pana who had overheard our trouble. "Vanessa Pana, how could we manage without you?" we all thanked her. I mean, she can be quite generous. If Delilah Mara would have come, we may still have been stuck trying to decipher the license plate. I placed the magnifying glass over the photo and our answers were revealed. The SUV's license plate read: 419-O-A23-FUN. Above this pattern were a few short words: U.S. Circus!

"I think I remember that circus! When the Feline & K9 Companions were first solving their mystery last month, they found out that the one who took their club's cat was Gracie McCarthy, a performer and former acrobat of that circus! I've heard that she and Vanessa McAtee have been close friends for a long time. Vanessa McAtee also knew Gracie McCarthy's niece, Jane! People say Jane isn't her original name. It's actually Jessica," Royal Romeo revealed. "Now I get it!" I exclaimed happily. "So that must mean that Gracie McCarthy is related to Jessica!" gasped Royal Romeo. Everyone was shocked at Royal Romeo's conclusions, including Mr. Louis. The rest of the way, hardly anyone spoke.

We were all concentrated on the music which was being played on the radio. It was a song by Jump 5 called "Shining Star." Two hours later, we reached our final destination: The Sacramento Adventure. It wasn't as large of a building as the Prehistoric Museum in San Francisco. The truth was, it had only 2 floors plus an underground floor. We immediately parked our car.

"Do you think the red SUV is here?" I asked. "I don't know. But maybe we could scan the first four rows of this parking lot," suggested Mr. Louis. "But we better hurry. It's 2:00 p.m. and we should not waste a bit of time on the search," Vanessa Pana reminded for she had brought her watch.

We went through the parking lot and found a total of three SUV's. The first one wasn't it; the second one had the same license number, but not the word "fun." The last one was the exact same number as the second SUV. Except it had the word FUN included. "So this is the SUV!" I said surprised. "I thought they might be," predicted Royal Romeo. "Let's not waste time! We must find Vanessa McAtee and Jessica!" Vanessa Pana interrupted. I know I said the museum "looks" smaller than the one near my home, but inside, it looks like a dome. After we purchased tickets and received a map of the museum, we were on our way. The meteorites must be on the bottom floor, we thought. When I mentioned that the museum had two floors, I meant to say that the second floor was underground. Back to the subject for now! To travel faster, we took an elevator. Today, not so many people had come to the museum. So that made our investigation not so hard after all!

2:30 p.m. (later)

The bottom floor was huge with halls, exhibits, and lots of surprises at every corner. It took a lot of time, but while we were walking through an exhibit of igneous rocks, I spotted a familiar person. I walked away from my friends to get a closer look. Oh my goodness, it's a monument, it's a fossil, it's JESSICA, Gracie McCarthy's niece! But where was Vanessa McAtee? Aw, never mind. For now, we'll concentrate on our suspect. I looked at the few people in the museum. How could they just walk around and mind their own business without realizing there's a criminal nearby? I knew this was my only chance to save the pre historic museum. So I called over Vanessa Pana, Royal Romeo, and Mr. Louis. They too, saw that one of our thieves was on the loose! "Let's follow her!" Royal Romeo spoke up when he saw that everyone else was silent. "We might as well. She may lead us to Miss McAtee," agreed Mr. Louis.

As we trailed after Jessica, we tried not to act as suspicious as we could. We didn't want Jessica to start suspecting that something was going on and she was being followed.

During our trio, we went through two hallways, one exhibit, and a door that Jessica passed through, I could tell by Mr.

Louis's heavy breathing and our loud pants that this was extremely tiring.

Behind the door Jessica passed through, we saw an exhibit with a gate that guarded the, "The Rare Gifts Exhibit." Mr. Louis showed his admission tickets and we were let in and shown inside a highly decorated room with lights that reflected on beautiful jewels and valuable treasures from countries all around the world. One item I recognized was a marble dragon from China. I once saw it in a magazine a couple of days ago.

"All we need to do is find four meteorites and our two thieves," Royal Romeo gladly stated. The rest of us agreed and knew that the meteorites were definitely going to be around here somewhere. We just knew it! "But the big question is, where did Jessica go?" asked Vanessa Pana. "Good question!" I cried as I rapidly glanced around the exhibit hoping to still see Jessica there. But sadly, there was no sign of her anywhere! We might as well start searching all over again.

"Let's split up into groups so we can cover more ground," Vanessa Pana suggested. "Okay, I guess that could be done. But I want us all back at the exhibit entrance at 5:00 p.m. sharp," Mr. Louis instructed. "I brought walkie-talkies so we can stay in touch and communicate," Vanessa Pana recalled. Wow, she is so prepared for everything! She reached in her bag for the requested items. Mr. Louis and Royal Romeo would be in one group while Vanessa Pana and I would be in the other. We had made up our minds that Group 1 would search for Jessica and Vanessa McAtee while Group 2 would try to recover the meteorites. Vanessa Pana and I looked at the museum map. Vanessa Pana spotted a section in the exhibit called, "Universal Sights."

"It must have something to do with outer space," I joked. We looked over the map again, but found nothing else helpful for our search. "If your guess is correct, the meteorites are probably in there," Vanessa Pana predicted. We were currently at the exhibit's entrance. All we need to do was follow these directions:

1. Go to Section # 3

2. Find a hallway with fall decorations

3. Pass through a door and enter "Universal Sights."

"This shouldn't take long at all!" I reassured Vanessa Pana as we entered a doorway to Section 3 which revealed a colorful hallway with orange, red, and light brown colored wallpaper. On one side of the hallway were pumpkins, piles of hay, and jack o' lanterns.

"Wow! I guess they're going into Halloween and fall season a little early," Vanessa Pana told me. "It's more than just a LITTLE early, you know," I muttered. We burst our laughing at the thought and I accidentally bumped into a scarecrow. "Oh my goodness, Allie

Angie! You knocked the scarecrow off of one of the pumpkins!" Vanessa Pana laughed. "We might as well try to put it back in its place," I said trying to lift up the huge straw made structure.

3:15 p.m. (It's almost 5 p.m.!)

Vanessa Pana and I were finally able to place the scarecrow back to its original position. After the last push, we managed to lean the scarecrow carefully against the wall on the pumpkin without having it topple all over again. Just then, a handkerchief fell out of one of the scarecrow's pant legs. Vanessa Pana and I looked at it for a couple of minutes. The handkerchief was white with soft, fancy, pink lace sewn on all edges!

We figured out that this piece of cloth contained something! The handkerchief was tied together with a long strand of red ribbon. With strong effort, I was able to cut the ribbon to reveal two mysterious objects: a note and a silver key!

"This is cool! I wonder what the key opens!" exclaimed Vanessa Pana. "These items remind me of something. You know what Marie Roberts said about the key? It is in something dressed in hay, looks like a human, and is despised by birds. This key must lead to the missing gemstones!" I revealed. "You do have a smart point here. Let's read the note. It might give us a clue!" suggested Vanessa Pana. I laid the note flat on the red checked, carpeted floor and read aloud:

"Ye who find this key must go to an exhibit which has been robbed. Near it, is a scientific fossil room. One out of five choices has the key's leading treasures. But beware!!!! This choice has not been opened in years, possibly decades. Hence it will bring guarding creatures which may frighten you. P.S. to the death: Hope you love dead creatures. You will see many and more than you have seen alive. HA HA HA HA!!!!

Chapter 8: Faraway Destination

The last line of the note made our bodies shiver. "We must give this to the rest of the club when we return home," Vanessa Pana warned.

Chapter 9: The Mystery Closet

Part V: Pierre

While our three lucky detectives were away, the rest of the club sat in the living room, bored. Mrs. Louis had gone to work and there wasn't much to do. I tried entertaining everyone with poems, jokes, and magic tricks, but nothing really seemed to work.

"Why don't we go to the museum and see if we can find any more clues. I mean, we can make another investigation if we want," I finally suggested to our remaining, present club members. "But Mrs. Louis is at work and she doesn't want us to leave the apartment unsupervised," warned Delilah Mara. "You know how Allie Angie wrote Marie Roberts's hints to the gemstones on her notepad? I think we should look for it and use the information to unlock the secret place where the gemstones are supposedly hidden. We know the gemstones are probably in the museum. But we first need to find out where," I announced.

At that moment, everyone's frowns turned upside down. Ok, maybe not completely upside down, but there were still a couple of puzzled expressions. Hopefully the rest of my friends were eager to continue solving our mystery. We just couldn't give up yet.

"I think the notepad is in the bathroom somewhere," Syleria Susae predicted. We hurried over to the bathroom and searched. I sniffed every spot, but found nothing much: 2 squished spiders and 3 live ones, 4 bars of old soap, 1 extra roll of rainbow colored toilet paper, 7 green two headed beetles (I didn't even know those existed.), and a couple of helpless flies in spider webs screaming for help (no one bothered to help them, by the way).

Our last place we checked was behind the toilet. There was Allie Angie's notepad! But it was all covered in gray dusty smelling moth balls. "Why don't you go retrieve it?" asked Delilah Mara. "Ew! I'm not going near that disgusting glob of stuff," I complained. In the end, Mario Marco settled down the argument.

"Let's find a broom or a brush to dust off the notepad," he suggested. I'm glad Mario Marco stayed with us. If he was not around, this fight might have been going on for quite a while. After being in the kitchen for almost half an hour, we turned up with an old paintbrush. It wasn't much, but at least it might come in handy. Syleria Susae, Mario Marco, and Delilah Mara dusted all the globs of lint, dead insects, and spider webs off the poor innocent notepad.

Allie Angie's notepad has a red velvet color on the front and is used only on special occasions. Allie had gotten it for a welcome home present when she was adopted by our next door neighbors. I opened it to the first few pages and read:

"Look for something full of hay, is dressed like a human, and is despised by birds. The key is inside. Go to a place where fossils are prepared for going out on display. The key is south in a building that Gracie McCarthy's friend knows a lot about."

"The key is probably in Sacramento. But I'm wondering if the gemstones are near our county. Well, there is a fossil preparation lab near the Valuable Rocks Exhibit. Maybe . . . just maybe, there could be a chance that the finding of the gemstones may be restored," I thought. I gathered everyone to the living room and I discussed my prediction. But just like Mario Marco's first time experience, nobody had the strength to believe me. With tremendous effort, I still insisted on going to the museum for a last time, quick scan investigation.

Quietly as we could, we crept our of our apartment room hoping not to be seen. Walking down the hallway, we saw a staircase, and further down the endless looking hallway was an elevator. Just as we were about to hop down the first few stairs, we heard a door unlock. The door was right next to the staircase. Since the staircase was on our left, we hurried over to the right side of the hallway to the elevator that was up ahead. We passed seven apartment doors and doubted that we would make it to hiding.

Delilah Mara pushed the elevator button rapidly over and over again. The transporter's doors slowly opened and we jammed ourselves inside. The door next to the staircase slowly opened and we heard heavy footsteps heading our way. Uh oh, we were in terribly big trouble! The elevator doors were still wide open and everyone feared of being seen. Syleria Susae didn't take any chances as she hit the accelerate button on the elevator. At first the elevator started to move and the doors were still OPEN!!!! "Syleria Susae, you forgot to push the "door close" button. We all panicked and without wasting time,

Chapter 9: The Mystery Closet

Syleria Susae hurried over and pressed the correct button. The elevator stopped still in its tracks and it made a loud noise. We all yelped in terror and then the elevator doors slammed closed and shut at last. After a few minutes, we landed on the first floor with an extremely loud thud.

We were able to reach the first floor safely. "Whew, that was a close one," sighed Gabriel Gordon with relief. Next, we walked a few blocks and settled ourselves on a bus for a quicker ride. It was going to be 3:00 p.m. and Mrs. Louis would be back at 4:45 p.m. So there wasn't much time for us to make our investigation in shorter times. Luckily, Gabriel Gordon and I packed some gear.

I had a small bag around my neck which contained a camera, Allie Angie's notepad, a flashlight, a cell phone, and other items which may come to our use. As we made our way to the Valuable Rocks Exhibit, I started looking around for a fossil preparation lab. There was nothing in sight that seemed to match my descriptions.

"Let's go through the exhibit. We may find something," suggested Mario Marco. As we scanned our environment, Delilah Mara spotted a door near a balcony which read: EMPLOYEES ONLY!!!

She signaled for the rest of us to follow her and we ended up finding ourselves in a strange environment. We were in some sort of science lab! But not just any lab, but a fossil preparation lab! People dressed in white lab coats were using microscopes, tools, and magnifying glasses to study ancient dinosaur bones. The club members gathered around under a table and we talked about the rest of our search.

"The gemstones should be around here somewhere. So why don't we look in unsuspected places like cabinets, closets, boxed crates, or anything that looks like a good hiding place for the gemstones," I instructed. "Good idea!" everyone

cheered. That's exactly what we
did.

We started to search up, down,
and all around. But we came up
with nothing. We explored the last
section of the fossil lab and
located a small closet. Since the
door was unlocked we opened it to
reveal nothing but shelves full of
lab tools. "It's okay, Pierre. It
was worth a try looking for a clue
anyway," comforted Gabriel Gordon
when he saw my disappointed look.
"I knew all of this was a waste of
time. It's going to be 4:00 p.m.
and Mrs. Louis will be arriving
home form work soon!" complained
Delilah Mara. "Don't blame Pierre.
He was only trying to help,"
Syleria Susae recalled as she
tried to reason with Delilah Mara.
As they both continued to argue. I
thought about the closet for a few
seconds. The gemstones had to be
around here somewhere. I grabbed a
flashlight and started inspecting
the closet's special features,
with the other few club members
eyeing me curiously.

Chapter 9: The Mystery Closet

They knew that I wasn't going to give up just yet. The closet was more like a small room. It had a huge photo frame of a famous geologist which covered a portion of the wall. There were also two big bookcases, and two pieces of furniture: a large wardrobe and a stack of wooden boxes. What was peculiar was that these were all leaning against the wall! The floor was made of wooden boards that were each shaped like planks. Whenever I stepped near the photo frame, the wooden boxes, the large wardrobe, or the bookcases, I would hear a faint echo or a hollow sounding creak.

Mario Marco and Gabriel Gordon must have also noticed that because they both commented, "It sounds hollow behind all these objects. Do you think we should see what's behind them?" I agreed and so did everyone else except Delilah Mara who didn't volunteer to help us much, anyway. It took at least 10 minutes to move everything, but lastly we moved all objects to one side of the small room. To me, it looked bigger than your average sized closet. When we finished we saw an awed expression on Delilah Mara's face. I thought she was impressed on how we moved the huge furniture, but the fact was, they weren't so heavy.

But no, she was actually staring at the wall which revealed five small doors about the size of your average sixth grader. I'm pretty sure about that because of Mr. and Mrs. Louis's niece, Sadie Dawes who is about 11 or 12 years old. I don't remember much of what she looks like, but I'll never forget a person's height measurements. Everyone else turned around and saw the five doors.

The first door led to a closet that revealed a collection of dead rats, moles, and opossums. We just could NOT stand the smell of these creatures. The second door led to a spooky tunnel that contained dead insects and live ones too. We were practically screaming the whole way. The tunnel ended at the entrance of the third door. The fourth door led to a basement which had cans of money. Most were old torn bills that probably weren't worth anything. There were dead creatures lying on the ground and hanging on the ceiling. In particular, we were scared to death when we saw this dead lion hanging on the ceiling and a beheaded chicken. But surprisingly the last door was locked! It had a key hole, so a key must be found to open it. When Syleria Susae mentioned on trying to find the key, Delilah Mara objected, "It's 4:25 p.m.! We need to get back home before Mrs. Louis finds out that we're missing!"

For once I understood that Delilah Mara was right. I think having the gemstones and meteorites stolen and missing was enough for us to handle. But having US missing was a whole different matter. On our run all the way home, most of us seemed extremely quiet. I knew that our club members didn't want to give this investigation a rest either. Hopefully, we may turn up with enough clues to aid us for our find of the missing key!

Chapter 10: The Valuable Find

Part VI: Allie Angie

3:30 p.m. (Sacramento Adventure)

Vanessa Pana and I hurried to Universal Sights as fast as we could. We opened a door and smack in the front of us was an enormous display stand covered by a large glass squared structure or a cube which protected and guarded . . . the four lost meteorites! They were found at last! Vanessa Pana and I gasped in shock, unable to speak.

For a few minutes, we studied the meteorites. They were polished and clean, that's what it seemed. "I guess Jessica and Vanessa McAtee took extra care of these meteorites," I commented. "Of course they would! These are expensive!" exclaimed Vanessa Pana.

An unexpected ring of a telephone interrupted our deep thoughts. Near the meteorites was a telephone booth with a ringing telephone (obviously). When I answered it, I was surprised to hear Royal Romeo's voice on the other end of the line, "It looks like we've arrested Vanessa McAtee and Jessica." We caught them discussing a plan to nab the gemstones. To prove they were criminals, Mr. Louis showed the police the newspaper which contained Vanessa McAtee's photo of when she had gone missing from jail. I let them study the pictures I took on the night of the meteorite's robbery with Gabriel Gordon!" I exclaimed, "That's wonderful! Tell Mr. Louis to gather the police and go to Universal Sights. The meteorites are displayed in the exhibit."

Royal Romeo and Mr. Louis agreed to meet us at our current destination. It took a lot of hard work, but the police were finally able to break the glass structures around the meteorites. At the moment, Vanessa Pana rushed over to the telephone booth and called our club members. They too, were delighted at the story of the valuable finding! She also mentioned the mystery key, which caused more excitement between the club members.

"That key just might lead us to the other half of the mystery. When you guys come home, we'll explain what we're planning to do with that key and the manuscript you found in the handkerchief," instructed Pierre who was now on the other side of the line.

Moreover, our mystery was not over yet. Even though we restored the finding of the lost meteorites, we still needed a further investigation for the lost gemstones that Marie Roberts stole. We frequently needed to find them before Marie Roberts gives them to some retailer, sells them, or escapes with them. What we need to know was: 1-What does the key open?, 2-Where are the gemstones?, 3-Where does Marie Roberts live?

With extreme desperation, we just might be able to uncover this information.

Part VII: Mario Marco – 6 p.m.

Our three absent members arrived back home and we threw them a celebration! Syleria Susae also told Mrs. Louis about the findings of the five unusual closets. Mrs. Louis didn't seem mad at all, but rather impressed! Whew, that was a really close one! But I think the most exciting part about today was going back to the museum. After a quick supper, we all went to the Prehistoric Museum. Since today was a special celebration for the manager, the museum wouldn't close until 8:00 p.m.

With the mystery key in paws and the manuscript in our care, we would surely discover our last clues in the secret closets. On our drive, I quietly went through Delilah Mara's secret notebook. At least she wasn't looking. Lately, she has been writing some pretty nice things about everyone:

MARIO MARCO HAS A SPECTACULAR AND INTELLIGENT PERSONALITY!

Chapter 10: The Valuable Find

SYLERIA SUSAE HAS A SHINY, WHITE,
CREAMY COAT!

VANESSA PANA AND ALLIE ANGIE ARE
THE BEST!!!!! (SO IS THE REST OF
THE CLUB!)

I quickly closed the notebook, as our vehicle reached a parking lot. "Here it goes," I thought. As I said a quiet prayer on our way inside the museum, something inside of me told that the mystery key that Vanessa Pana and Allie Angie had found and the secret closet with the doors had something to do with the gemstones. I hoped that prediction was correct, but I doubted it. That same question about the key and the doors echoed in my head over and over again. I thought this would go on forever. Thankfully it stopped when we reached the science lab in the Valuable Rocks Exhibit.

Chapter 11: The Closet's Special Secret

We reached the small room where the five doors were located. The museum manager and an employee accompanied us as the club showed Mr. and Mrs. Louis through the doors. The manager had no idea that the science lab contained a closet with five mysterious doors. Everyone was spooked and awed by every door's tunnel. I think Mrs. Louis was really eager to get this over with. When it came to the fifth door, the manager turned the knob, but it was evidently locked. Syleria Susae handed the manager the key and he fit it through the keyhole. As he worked the key in the lock, he commented, "I guess this door hasn't been used for years. No wonder this door can't open! But for one thing, I don't remember the museum containing secret tunnels and rooms."

The key worked in the end and Mrs. Louis gasped in amazement. "So the key did belong to this door. What a coincidence!"

exclaimed Mr. Louis with astonishment. The opened door revealed a descending staircase which led to a dark basement. I peered in to see, but light was not found to help us look at what lay ahead of the staircase. The employee hurried outside of the room to get a lantern. When he returned, one by one we went down the stairs with the manager in the lead. The stairway seemed to go on forever as we stepped down and down into the darkness. When we reached the bottom, we found ourselves in a dark room on a cemented floor.

Mrs. Louis spotted a light switch, which gave as much light as our lantern. With the light on, we saw the room which seemed really large. In front of us were desks, chairs, tables, a small kitchen, and unusual sights.

On one of the desks were papers. While everyone else explored the mysterious room, I began to study some of the room's features. At least there were no lifeless creatures lying around or else I

would just have run out of there.
The walls were plain white, but
had marks, holes, and scrapings of
paint to reveal ugly spots. But as
you can tell, this part of the
museum seemed to be extremely
ancient. On some parts of the
walls were newspaper clippings,
old and recent.

As I read them I became
suspicious. A couple of the
article titles read: "U.S.
CIRCUS'S PERFORMERS ARRESTED,"
"FELINE & K9 COMPANIONS GAIN
FAME!", and "GEMSTONES &
METEORITES UNDER ATTACK!" Did any
of this have to do with the stolen
gemstones? I studied the papers on
one of the desks.

What surprised me was that these
had to do with Marie Roberts! I
started looking around for the
gemstones and found out that they
weren't here! Pretty smart thief,
I thought. She must have taken the
gemstones with her! I read through
some of Marie Roberts's journal
entries, they claimed that Marie
Roberts was scheduled to have the
gemstones donated to the Field

Museum of Chicago! That would take place on the third day of August! Oh my goodness! Illinois was a few days away from here if your travel was by car.

What could we do? I dug around in one of the desk drawers hoping to find more clues of this information! As I took out some old postcards, I found a white card with fancy writing in print:

Marie Roberts
Employee of V. R. Exhibit
Alternate Meteorologist
Professional Biologist
Issued for June 12th
ID: 432176

Mr. Louis had seen what I was doing and asked the manager, "What is this?" He replied, "That's Marie Robert's I.D. card! She used to work here, but decided to retire for some unknown reason. Obviously she didn't do much in our museum exhibits. She only prepared fossils and gemstones for going out on display."

"When did she retire?" asked Mrs. Louis curiously. "Around June 12th, actually. She never was hired for that long," the manager continued. As Mrs. Louis continued to ask a couple of questions, I peered into the drawer to see a package of stamps . . . and an envelope with bold lettered handwriting: DO NOT READ: PRIVATE!!!! I opened the envelope and saw a paper with a message to Vanessa McAtee:

August 1st of 2006

To: Vanessa McAtee M. and Jessica, a further friend

From: Miss you know who

I am currently finding a way to sell off these stolen gemstones or so called securities for a large fee. Hopefully, this may cover at least a third of Gracie McCarthy's fine. If any questions call or mail to my home:

467 P.O. Box
San Francisco, California 417354

Or call this number: (417)-235-1403

Now this letter made sense! Marie Roberts took the gemstones with her instead of hiding them here because she probably knew Vanessa McAtee was going to find the key somehow, which she didn't. Marie Roberts was planning to later come back with the key and mail this letter. But as it turns out, we find the key and she can't get back to her secret place which is in the fifth door!

"Mr. Louis, take a look at this!" I called. Mr. Louis took the letter to the manager. "This should definitely lead us to the gemstones without a doubt! Why, I never knew Marie Roberts would do such a thing! We must arrest her as soon as possible!" bellowed Mr. Louis. "But what about the museum's festival at the end of the month?" Mrs. Louis cried. "I'm afraid we'll have to move it to another date or cancel it," the manager sighed. "This is horrible! What are we are we going to do?" asked Gabriel Gordon. "I know! We can't leave the museum in great distress," groaned Pierre. "If we can, we must find those gemstones," declared Royal Romeo. And that's what we agreed to do!

Chapter 12: The Big Chase

Part VIII: Gabriel Gordon

It was July 29th and the festival would take place the day after tomorrow. So now we had less than 24 hours. Early at 4:30 a.m., I looked up Marie Roberts's address in the internet which gave me results and specific directions. "This will be a piece of cake," I thought. Well, maybe beef since cake contains too much sugar.

I found out that Marie Roberts didn't live too far away. At 8:24 a.m., I told Royal Romeo and Delilah Mara about my plan to go to Marie Roberts's house and retrieve the gemstones. At 9:00 a.m., we quietly snuck out the door, but Mrs. Louis had seen us and she followed on our way out and curiously asked, "Where are you guys headed?" I thought of a quick excuse and lied, "Outside to get some fresh air. We had trouble breathing last night in our room." I knew I was being dishonest, but it was the only way to get those gemstones back! We passed by streets, roads, parks, and yards. Delilah Mara had a bag to put the gemstones in and she kept it wrapped around her tail. Royal Romeo had tied a watch to his leg to keep track of time, and last but not least, was a cell phone strapped on my collar in case we needed to call for help.

In about 20 minutes, we found Marie Roberts's house. It surprised me to see it was only one story, but was quite long in length according to my predictive measurements. We detectives searched around the house, trying to find a way inside.

The house didn't seem old at least, but quite new! The walls of the house were beige and the roof was tiled with a light brick red. Too bad we couldn't peek inside the windows because all the blinds and shades were closed. Delilah Mara spotted some basement windows near the ground of the house. We looked in, but only saw blackness. "Oh great, now what are we going to do?" asked Royal Romeo helplessly. "We need to think of a way to get inside, but how?" wondered Delilah Mara. My eyes drifted off to an old shed behind Marie Roberts's house and a trashcan beside the garage.

Since the trashcan didn't have a lid, I saw a moldy and crumply pizza box lying on layers of trash. All this gave me an idea! "Delilah Mara, go get that pizza box in the trashcan!" I commanded. "But that box is in garbage! I don't want to become contagious, you know," Delilah Mara complained. "I have a plan and it won't work unless we use that pizza box!" I remarked. "Ok, fine! Whatever it takes to get those gemstones back," she muttered as she stomped all the way to the smelly trash barrel. When she came back, we hurried over to the old shed. The shed's door was a crack open and we snuck inside. What stood before us caught our eyes. There were shelves, walls, and a table of beautiful artwork.

Chapter 12: The Big Chase

"This must be what Marie Roberts does to pass the time. Probably a hobby or an activity of some sort," I guessed. Royal Romeo and Delilah Mara nodded, but were too excited to speak. On the desks and shelves were sculptures, clay, moldings, paints, oil pastels, pencils, paper, and various materials. The wall was decorated with realistic masks, scarecrows, and art contest certificates.

"Marie Roberts must have been some professional artist," I stated. "Probably so. Look at how she sculpts things!" exclaimed Royal Romeo. "Well, she's a jewel thief just the same anyway," Delilah Mara reminded.

There seemed to be nothing in the shed that would work with my plan. I was about to go when smack on the top of the door was a nail that had a hanger which held a shirt, shoes, a cap, and overalls. This was exactly what I was looking for! "Delilah Mara, Royal Romeo, these clothes will be perfect for my plan!" I exclaimed. "What IS your plan?" asked Royal

120

Romeo. "I was thinking. Since Marie Roberts is probably still home, two of us could dress in the clothes and use two broomsticks to put in the pants of the overalls for balance, like stilts. The shoes could be put at the base of the broomsticks. Then one of us will wear the cap and put their paws through the sleeves and wear a mask. The dog at the bottom will be carrying the dog who's wearing the mask. Are you guys starting to get what I'm saying?" I instructed. "It's like the top dog!" cheered Delilah Mara. "Then the dog at the top will hold the pizza box," I continued. "Oh, now I get it! You want two of us to ring Marie Roberts's doorbell and try to get in her house using disguises," said Royal Romeo.

We got our stuff outside. Then we tried as bravely as we could to step up to Marie Roberts's porch. Delilah Mara and I would be the ones in disguise while Royal Romeo would hide behind a nearby bush which was also part of my plan. With a trembling paw, I pushed the doorbell and it sounded off with an echoing ring. "Here it goes," I heard Delilah Mara whisper with a lump in her throat.

The door quickly opened before I knew it and Marie Roberts appeared before us. Now I have never seen her up close or face to face, but believe me, I could feel the butterflies in my stomach. Her eyes were shadowed with hatred, greed, and evil.

"Excuse me sir, but I'm afraid I didn't order a pizza," she snapped. Just then, Royal Romeo galloped straight at Marie Roberts and pulled on her pant leg while Delilah Mara and I jumped out of our disguises and raced inside the house. This caused Marie Roberts to just totally explode and scream like crazy! For a moment, I thought I might go deaf if she didn't shut up right away.

The big chase was confusing because we all split up and raced away in separate directions. Marie Roberts could have split in three parts, but luckily she didn't. I could just see those fumes puffing out of her brain. While I was scampering around the house, I wondered where my friends had gone, but I just tried to find the gemstones, wherever they were. In the end, my plan turned into practically a dorky mess! Call me insane if you like. First, I skidded across the room and knocked over a chair, which hit a table, that leaned against a stack of dishes on the kitchen counter, and that led to a mess on the floor. Dishes crashed to the ground with loud shatters. This caused some nearby vases to crack and crumble away. I thought that was cool. I never knew about such sound effects. The things and food on the table was also knocked over. What a tremendous crash!

The floor was now covered with furniture, glass, eggs, ham, and a spilled gallon of milk. I bet that caught Marie Roberts's attention because then she stepped into the kitchen and yelled with anger and what was worse enough, she practically started cussing all over the place. How dare she shout in my poor innocent ears that have

never heard things like that
before. The next minute, she was
grabbing a broom and gave a start
after me. I dodged room after room
avoiding furniture, objects, and
food the broom struck. I ran near
a desk and the broom struck a
phone instead of me. Believe me,
that was a close one! I turned to
run, but one of my legs was stuck
in the telephone's cords. At that
point, Royal Romeo sprung from
behind a couch and pinched Marie
Roberts's arm tightly with his
fangs.

I quickly was able to loosen the
cords and made my escape. Delilah
Mara passed me and headed toward
an open door in the distance. It
sure didn't lead outside, but in a
basement at the bottom of Marie
Roberts's house. It was pitch
black down there and hard to see.
For once in my life, I wish I was
a cat. The basement had a lot of
junk such as old boxes, bicycles,
tools, and a wardrobe near some
hanging jackets. Since there was
still a bit of light, I saw some
shiny objects inside near a corner

of the wardrobe. They were . . .
the gemstones!

Since there were lots of coats
hanging, it was hard to get in the
wardrobe to the back and retrieve
the gemstones. Delilah Mara and I
closed the wardrobe doors. Then
she put the precious treasures in
her bag, but all of a sudden the
wardrobe doors opened and Marie
Roberts stood before us. She
didn't see me because I was
covered by a row of black dresses.
Since my fur was black, I blended
in easily. But poor silver colored
Delilah Mara was seen as visible.
I would just hate to be in her
paws.

Marie Roberts reached for
Delilah Mara and put her in the
bag saying, "Helping me steal the
gemstones are you? Your only
reward will be staying at a dog
pound in Chicago!" With bag in
hand, Marie Roberts walked off
commenting, "I might as well get
ready for my trip." Marie Roberts
disappeared up the basement stairs
and locked the door! Oh no, I was
trapped! How would I ever get out?

I searched through the basement
and turned on a light switch. The
basement did have 3 windows! Maybe
I could find a way to get to one
of them! I hopped on a chair, then
a desk, and above some boxes to
see an unlocked window which was
opened about a crack!

I softly and carefully hopped on
one box after another. Little by
little, I pushed the window open
trying not to make the boxes
wobble. I squeezed out the window
and stepped on warm grass. Yea, I
made it out alive!

As quickly as I could, I hid
behind a bush. At the moment,
Marie Roberts came out of the
house with the bag and with
Delilah Mara and the gemstones in
it! Just then, I felt a tap on my
shoulder. I jumped and turned
around to see Royal Romeo! "You
take the cell phone, Gabriel
Gordon and follow Marie Roberts to
accompany Delilah Mara and see
where Marie Roberts is heading.
I'll run home and tell our owners
what happened. Hopefully they'll
be able to have the police arrest

Marie Roberts in Chicago," he said. Before I could say anything else, he ran off to the direction of home. Home was where I so badly wanted to go. I didn't want to follow Marie Roberts. What if I was the next one caught?

I knew it would do no good just standing here, so I took no time to waste and I hopped in the trunk of Marie Roberts's car where Delilah Mara and the gemstones were currently being held as captives. Into the bag I went just as Marie Roberts put a suitcase in the trunk and shut the door. As Marie Roberts's car started to head out of town, I made sure Delilah Mara was okay, which she was.

Then I used the cell phone to call home. Mr. Louis promised to send the police to Chicago right away. The rest of the day was spent with staying in the car for about an hour. After that, I felt Marie Roberts pick up the bag. I hope she didn't realize that I was also in it. Well I only heard her mutter on how the bag seemed a little heavier than usual. "That unintelligent, overweight dog! She'll end up making a hole in this bag and then my robbery will be revealed!" she complained.

I tried as hard as I could to make out where I was, but nothing seemed to help! All I heard were cars and people. "We must be in some sort of city," thought Delilah Mara. Before I could realize it I heard Marie Roberts mutter, "Time to empty this dweeby bag!" and the bag we were in was turned completely upside-down with Delilah Mara and the gemstones piled on top of me. I desperately started gasping for breath. "Do you think we're in Chicago?" asked Delilah Mara. "No way, Chicago is far, far away from California and practically across the country!" I replied. Then, I felt the bag open and out plopped me, Delilah Mara, and the gemstones crashing on my head. Ow. Ow. And Double Ow!

"Aha, I was wondering what was making this bag heavy and now I know what! Now I can hold two puppies for ransom!" she cackled.

Marie Roberts grabbed us and dumped us both in separate cages. By this time, I saw that we had arrived at the Los Angeles Airport! We were barely leaving California! Marie Roberts gathered all the gemstones and put them in her suitcase. Our cages were placed on a conveyor belt and so was the suitcase.

We went through a dark tunnel and in another room where luggage was being sorted out. An employee put us near a pile of luggage that was scheduled to go to Illinois. Delilah Mara and I tried banging on our cages, but it was no use. We would never be able to escape!

Later at 11:55 a.m., we were put on board of an airplane. About three hours later we reached Chicago, Illinois. Delilah Mara and I, along with the suitcase were placed on another conveyor belt where we were placed near another pile of luggage. I could tell that Delilah Mara was feeling sick and her face was turning green. I actually thought she was going to barf.

There wasn't much we could do, so we started whimpering in distress. What completely surprised us was that a small Terrier came up to us and asked what was wrong. I explained to the Terrier that we were kidnapped and that we needed to get back to San Francisco, California. The Terrier introduced herself as Amber; a working dog used to sniff out any harmful drugs in the luggage, but was glad to help us get home.

Amber was able to push our cages and the suitcase to another pile of luggage (luggage to California). We thanked Amber for her help but she just said, "I'll be glad to help! That's what working dogs are for!"

At 2:25 p.m., we were put on another conveyor belt (I don't know when this would ever end!) and onto a plane. Four hours later, we arrived back at the Los Angeles Airport. With great effort, I was able to bang my cage and get it open at last! The cage's lock had become sort of loose because of so much movement in the plane ride. Now that I was free, I unlocked Delilah Mara's suitcase and went to find a telephone booth. Marie Roberts had taken my cell phone so now I had no way to communicate with my family and friends.

On our way to a nearby phone booth, Delilah Mara had found a quarter on the ground which we used to pay for the phone call. It was now 6:30 p.m. when I called Mr. Louis. He was so overjoyed that he could barely speak. He told us that the police were able to arrest Marie Roberts earlier that day. He was even more excited when we told him we had the gemstones with us. "This is totally unbelievable!" Mr. Louis exclaimed. "It looks like the museum's festival won't be canceled after all!" Delilah Mara exclaimed. "You're right, Delilah Mara! The day after tomorrow we'll go to the festival!" announced Mr. Louis.

When we finally arrived home, there was hugging, cheering, crying (from Mrs. Louis), and food for Delilah Mara and I. We hadn't eaten anything this whole entire day and boy was I starved! After supper, I showed everyone the gemstones. Everyone awed and stared at the beauty of those gleaming gemstones like the diamonds, rubies, and emeralds. The most exciting part was when Delilah Mara, Royal Romeo, and I retold the story of the day's adventure. A lot of questions were asked, especially from Mr. and Mrs. Louis. You can tell that they really cared a lot for us!

Chapter 13: The Festival's Surprise

The day is finally here! Today is July 31st, the last day of the month AND also the date of the festival celebration! Before we went to the museum, we decided to watch the news and see what the weather was like for today. But instead of seeing the usual weather channel, we saw a news show about US! A broadcaster named Shiloh Donavan, a tall brown haired lady announced, "The gemstones have been finally found and so have the meteorites which were rescued by the Louis Family and their Bold Canine Companions. The museum's festival will offer a reward to those detectives."

At that very second, we all cheered and jeered like crazy! At two in the afternoon, we hopped in our car and set off for the Prehistoric Museum! When we arrived, we saw crowds of people encoring and holding up signs. "I can't believe it! We have fans!" screamed Vanessa Pana with delight. "And they've come to congratulate us!" continued Allie Angie. We spent the first few minutes answering questions from reporters and then we joined in with the festival! While we settled in for some dessert, Pierre spotted a familiar purple vehicle. A purple van came in parking and everyone gathered around to see who it was. But I think everyone already knew, for out of the vehicle came . . . THE FELINE & K9 COMPANIONS themselves!!!!! Sophie LeLaine, the main leader of the group stepped up and said, "I would like to thank the Dream Detectives Dog Club for saving the Prehistoric Museum while we professional sleuths were absent from detective work!"

Everyone applauded and fans yelled. I think the best part about today was that we got to meet every member from the most famous junior Californian detective groups! I've heard about their wonderful adventures, but have never seen the sleuths up close before. What I know now is that they're extremely smart and nice! My favorite member from the group is Panda Perry or aka: Panda. I have now appointed him as my role model. I later did get acquainted with him and he sure is one cool cat! Syleria Susae's new role model is Patience, the feline leader of the club, also known as vice president of the group. Patience, as I've heard is an intelligent Siamese cat who's claimed to come from a line of well bred champions on her mother's side. In interviews, it was her great, great grandmother who made her generation known actually.

Favorite Member/Role Model Picks:

Syleria Susae - Patience
Mario Marco - Hunter
Vanessa Pana - Jackson
Delilah Mara - Sheryl Star
Pierre - Naunee
Royal Romeo - Halloween
Allie Angie - Rosie
Gabriel Gordon - Panda Perry

For the rest of the day, we spent time with the Feline & K9 Companions. When it was 9:00 p.m., the museum showered off fireworks and music, plus a lot of cool stuff! The museum was even able to set up a carnival outside near the parking lot! The carnival included rides, food, bounce houses, and a huge slide!

In the end, Panda Perry gave me his email address and phone number! "Call me if you want to talk or need advice," he suggested with a grin. When it came time for us to leave and part ways, Panda gave me a detective journal with information. "It might help you if you need any tips. It obviously helped me as you can see," he said. "Wow, Panda! You really influence me," I answered as we shook paws. "So long, Shirley Detective!" he called as he ran off to join Sadie Dawes, his owner. Then I ran off to be with my own friends.

As we were climbing into our car, I went to the backseat and looked inside the detective journal that Panda Perry gave me. On the first page, were signatures

autographed from the famous young
detectives themselves!

Feline & K9 Companion Club:
Sophie LeLaine, Sadie Dawes,
Christy Norman, Dana Fryman,
Patience, Hunter, Halloween,
Rosie, Panda Perry, Naunee,
Penelope, Lola, Lassie, Buddy,
Jackson, Sheryl Star, Jazzy
Dancer, Bella

"Whoa!" I whispered in awe and
continued, "I can't wait for a new
mystery. Everyday comes in
different ways and I guess the
same goes for a mystery." I turned
to look out the window and spotted
the Feline & K9 Companions driving
away in their vehicle. Panda Perry
was in the passenger seat in the
front of the van, sitting on
Sadie's lap with his other feline
friend, Rosie. But that cat poked
his head out the window and waved
at me! I was sad to see them go.
Delilah Mara must have noticed my
sadness because she reassured me
not to worry. Her cousin, Jackson
may come to visit someday and
hopefully, he may bring some of
his club members. I hoped she was

right, since I was so eager to see Panda Perry again. But who knows? He will eventually have another mystery to solve. The same goes for us dog detectives too. But like Delilah Mara said, we'll see them again and I know we will.

THE END

Don't worry we'll be back again to tell you more about our adventures! But for now, let's settle down a bit. This may seem like the end of our story, but the truth is, you've only experienced the beginning of what it's like to be a canine sleuth!

Hope you enjoyed this!

Sincerely, Gabriel Gordon

OFFICIALLY: THE END

(Or is it just the beginning of ??? . . .)

A Word from the Author

Dear Reader,

You have just read my 3rd published book and the 2nd sequel of this series: The Dogs that follow their Detective Dreams. I was influenced by the Nancy Drew series to write this second novel of animal companion mystery and fun! I dedicate this book to my friends and the teamwork we share. Without them, this series would not have been born! This book was a continuation of what happened next after the Prehistoric Museum was robbed the first time. I thought it would be more interesting if I had characters influenced by the Feline & K9 Companions. So I introduced Sheryl Star's niece, Syleria Susae and Jackson's cousin Delilah Mara and their friends to solve the second robbery. This story is also dedicated to people who are easily influenced by others. Are you one of those people? I know I am!

Sincerely, Kitty/Sarah Cantu

About the Author

Sarah Veronica Cantu, otherwise known as Kitty K. Can 2 is 11 years old and was born in McAllen, Texas. When she was about 4 years old, she moved to Cincinnati, Ohio and before she began second grade, she moved again to Indianapolis, Indiana and attended Kingsway Christian School. Her origins are Hispanic, Italian, and a little bit of Asian. Her hair is black and eyes are brown. She is the oldest daughter of Ricardo and Veronica Cantu. Sarah has a little sister named Hannah, a brother named Jacob, and another brother named Richard. Her only pet is a one year old standard black female poodle whose full name is Syloria Quincy Rosaline Cantu (April 20th, 2005). Her best friends are Dana Kalachnick, Sarah Power, Amber

Roberts, Caitlin Needy, and Rachel Selke. Her hobbies are reading, writing, singing, and hanging out with friends. Her school hobbies are band and choir. Plus, her favorite sports are basketball, volleyball, and hockey. When she grows up she wants to be a cat/dog breeder, actress, singer, or writer, or maybe a couple or all of those!

Other Books by Sarah Cantu

The Dogs that Follow their Detective Dreams # 1: Find a New Home, 2nd edition

Coming Soon:

The Dogs that Follow their Detective Dreams # 3: Syleria Susae and Vanessa Pana's Unicorn Mystery

Similar Books:

The Feline & K9 Companions (a new series!)

www.ingramcontent.com/pod-product-compliance
Lightning Source LLC
Chambersburg PA
CBHW052146170626
46812CB00004B/1610